To

To Die In Vain

ASAD

**Lock Down Publications
& Ca$h Presents
To Die In Vain
A Novel by *ASAD***

ASAD

Lock Down Publications
P.O. Box 1482
Pine Lake, Ga 30072-1482

Visit our website at **www.lockdownpublications.com**

Cover design and layout by: Dynasty's Cover Me
Book interior design by: Shawn Walker
Edited by: Tumika Cain

Stay Connected with Us!

Text **LOCKDOWN** to 22828 to stay up-to-date with new releases, sneak peaks, contests and more…

Submission Guideline.

Submit the first three chapters of your completed manuscript to ldpsubmissions@gmail.com, subject line: Your book's title. The manuscript must be in a .doc file and sent as an attachment. Document should be in Times New Roman, double spaced and in size 12 font. Also, provide your synopsis and full contact information. If sending multiple submissions, they must each be in a separate email.

Have a story but no way to send it electronically? You can still submit to LDP/Ca$h Presents. Send in the first three chapters, written or typed, of your completed manuscript to:

LDP: Submissions Dept
Po Box 1482
Pine Lake, Ga 30072

DO NOT send original manuscript. Must be a duplicate.

Provide your synopsis and a cover letter containing your full contact information.

Thanks for considering LDP and Ca$h Presents.

ACKNOWLEDGEMENTS

I'm gonna keep this short and sweet, I thank God because I am still here after all the bullshit I have been through. I have to thank Ca$h and LDP for putting me on and doing what real niggas do, I got you from here. I thank everybody who is behind me because what we do I can't mention your names but you know who you are. To all the fuck niggas that plot my demise, this is your warning: my hands are dirty but my pistols area clean --- this ain't what you want!

Y'all better hope that this thing with LOCK DOWN PUBLICATIONS/THE NEW ERA keep me outta the streets. Because if I ever come back, your reign will end very gruesome.

To all of you who read my work, thanks for giving a hood dude a chance.

DEDICATION

This book is dedicated to those who have lost, and continue to lose, their lives for no reason. I pray you found peace in whatever comes after life.

ASAD

CHAPTER ONE

"Damn, baby, your lips are so soft," I whispered against her mouth while my hand journeyed underneath her shirt grazing her exposed nipple.

"Yea, you always say that when you want me to wrap my lips around something," she replied, chuckling.

I tried my best to give a wounded look of innocence, but the fact that she was holding the proof of my intentions firmly in her hand made keeping a straight face impossible.

"You make me sound so selfish," I said, kissing her neck gently, just the way she liked.

"No, baby, you're n...not selfish, but I wonder...if you could live without it."

I pulled back abruptly, horrified at just the thought that we might be taking a step backwards in the land of sexual experimentation. Melody and I have known each other since the sixth grade, and it had still taken me halfway through our freshman year of high school to see her topless! I was sensitive and understanding to the fact that she didn't view her body with the same beauty I did, but over the years I'd never wasted an opportunity to show her how I felt. Some dudes went for the size two cheerleader type, but that fragile look has never been my thang.

Melody was five foot six inches tall and carried her two hundred and ten pounds of curves with such unintentional sexiness that I couldn't stop my zipper from saluting whenever she was in the room. I'd found the weight room early in life so my five foot eleven inches and two hundred and eighty-five-pound frame wasn't something to be overlooked or underestimated. I needed a woman that looked like my woman and not my child or my little sister, so from early on Melody fit the bill.

When you factored in her inner beauty and intellect you could understand why she'd had my heart when it was just puppy love

I felt. Even though I'd showered her with attention and affection it still took years for her to come out of her shell and let me love her physically. I don't even want to put into words how long it took getting her comfortable in her own skin, but the comment she just made had me wondering how far we'd actually come.

"Live without it? Why would you say that, baby?"

"To see that look on your face," she replied laughing, squeezing my dick a little harder as she began moving her hand up and down.

"That ain't funny, Melody."

"Baby, giving you head costs me about five minutes out of my day, but that look on your face was priceless."

My retort was lost somewhere in the back of my throat, because the softness of her lips and the heat of her mouth had me pinned to the headboard of her bed. She'd been generous with her five minute estimate, because it felt like heaven wouldn't wait, but just as quickly, it was snatched away by the ringing of my phone.

"Isn't that your dad's ringtone?" she asked sitting up.

"Baby, don't stop," I pleaded. Her response was to cross her arms over her chest and stare me down, forcing me to pull the still ringing phone from my pocket.

"I can't explain to you how bad your timing is," I said by way of answering.

"Well, son, I believe it was you who wrecked your car and now are in need of a ride home. I'm in the neighborhood now, and no I'm not gonna wait for you to finish up whatever freak shit you're into at the moment."

"Come on, Pops, I…."

"*Now* Stephon," he said, disconnecting before I could get another word in.

Even though I was eighteen, and technically an adult, I rarely argued with my dad, but for the magic of Melody's mouth I'd come to blows with damn near anybody.

"We gotta hurry," I said, pulling her towards me.

"Boy stop, you think I didn't hear what your dad said."

"But, baby, I was almost there and...."

"Uh uh, because it wasn't just gonna be about you this time around," she said smiling.

"Really?"

"Really. So, we're gonna postpone this for the moment, and when we pick back up it better start off with you putting that thick ass tongue to use for something besides talking."

"Whatever you say, baby," I replied, taking her face in my hands and kissing her thoroughly. Before she could object I had my hand under her skirt and inside her panties, dipping my finger quickly inside her before pulling it out and licking her juices off.

"You so nasty."

"Only when it comes to you, and only because I love you," I replied with a wicked smile, fixing my clothing in anticipation of having to walk through her house. The last thing I needed was for her mom to literally catch me with my dick out. Between the both of her parents I considered her mom an ally, and even though we were both eighteen I didn't see how her having a visual of what I was doing to her little girl helped me in any way. Melody's father was a different story completely, because it didn't matter what I did or didn't do, I'd never be good enough for his daughter. At first, I'd thought it was because I'm black and they're white, but that notion was dispelled the first time they invited me over for dinner. I never really had a thing for white girls, but that was because I didn't see a lot of them where I came from. From the moment I had seen Melody she had my attention. The looks that we got or the under the breath comments that were made didn't matter. By now I was used to the hate, so I could've dealt with it from her parents, but that wasn't the vibe I got.

Then I thought it might be an economical class issue since I was born in D.C and they were from the suburbs of Virginia, but I never saw fear when they came to my neighborhood. The bottom line was that Melody was an only child, a daddy's girl, and no one would ever be good enough in his eyes. All I cared about was being good enough in hers though, and the way she was looking at me right now told me I had nothing to worry about.

"I love you too, Stephon. Tell your dad I said hi, and next time I'll drive you home."

"You know I don't want you in the streets of D.C. at night, babe. Besides I'll be getting my car fixed soon."

"We should just get a place together and...."

"Melody, we talked about this. We both need to be saving money for college, because it's only a few months before spring classes begin," I said patiently, trying to take the sting out of my voice while pulling her to her feet and into my arms.

"Baby, we can afford a one bedroom apartment. I mean I know your dad's paint business isn't exactly doing Wall Street numbers, but we both earn a decent living. And you know I can carry my own weight."

"It's not about that, sweetheart. I know I sound crazy by today's standards, but I wanna do things the right way when it comes to you. I ain't trying to just shack up."

"What are you saying?" she asked slowly.

"I'm saying I'ma make an honest woman out of you, and no that's not a proposal. I'm gonna do it way better than that."

"Ma...marriage?"

"I hope you didn't think I was in it just for the sex, Mel," I said laughing as she blushed a deep shade of red.

My ringing phone once again interrupted us, but instead of answering I laced her fingers with mine and led her from the room.

"Have a good evening, Mrs. Tyler," I called out as we passed her mom in the kitchen.

Before we even opened the front door, I could hear Smokey Robinson singing about cruising, which meant my father was parked right out front. It didn't matter how many times I told him not to play his music in this neighborhood, because he insisted nobody could argue with quality R&B.

"Will you call me when you get home?" she asked.

Once we were on her front porch I pulled her close to me and let our bodies sway to the rhythm of the music, humming in her ear before gently taking the lobe in between my lips and sucking hard enough to stop her breath.

"You know I'm gonna call you, babe, and we'll Facetime like we do every night."

"I'll be naked and waiting," she replied, standing on her tip-toes to kiss me one last time.

Our separation was equally reluctant, and it was moments like this that had me reconsidering the whole idea of us moving in together. I didn't just want us to be a statistic like so many other teenagers playing house. I might've been born into that constant cycle, but my parents had instilled something different in me, which made me want better for us. Shit, compared to all the people we knew that were our age, we were the only ones still using condoms!

"What's on your mind, boy?" my father asked once I was in the car.

Turning the music down so I wouldn't have to yell, I tried to figure out how to articulate what I was feeling. Me and my father had open communication. I mean I was his junior, so he understood me in ways my mom couldn't. What I loved most was that

he didn't judge me, regardless of what happened. He didn't sug-
arcoat shit, but even if he disagreed with me he'd still let me make
my own mistakes. His famous words were 'I can't live for you,'
but I still tried to ask myself what he would do before I made
important decisions. This point in my life was filled with important decisions.

"I love her, Pop."

"Okay, and?"

"Nah, I mean I really love her, like that forever type love."

"Forever, huh?" he questioned, turning the sound system
completely off and puffing on his trademark cigar thoroughly.

"Yeah, forever. It's damn near beyond words."

"How do you know it's that forever type of love, Stephon?"

"Because...loving her makes me a better man, it's not something I'm willing to live without. There's nothing that she does
for me that I couldn't get another woman to do, but it's only special because she does it. I love who she is as a person, and I'd do
anything for her, just like you would do for mom."

"That's not an easy road to travel, son. It takes dedication,
compromise, and sometimes the patience of a Tibet Monk."

"But in the end, it's worth it."

He nodded his head in affirmation of the truth, putting the
Mercedes into gear and pulling away from Melody's house. We
rode in silence for a couple blocks, but I caught him glancing my
way a time or two.

"You ready for the next step?" he asked casually.

"What do you mean?"

"Well, son, if you're being this introspective about the love
you have for Melody and using words like 'forever,' then it ain't
hard to figure out where this is headed."

"Do you think I'm ready, Pop?"

"That's not for me to decide, nor is it your mother's decision.
You're eighteen years old and that means any decisions you

14

make you will be accountable for. It's your life, so live it," he replied in between puffs of his cigar.

"I know it's my life, but man to man, do you think I'm ready?"

We came to a stop sign and sat there for a minute in silence. I felt a little uneasy, but I'd asked for the real and I knew that's what I would get no matter what.

"Yeah, you're ready," he replied, smiling at me and turning the radio back on.

We made it halfway through the next block before the roar of sirens and flashing lights caught both of our attention. A quick look in my side mirror revealed an unmarked cop car behind us signaling for us to pull over. Neither me or my father had any run ins with the law, but being black in this day in age came with a distrust for law enforcement. My parents had lived through the sixties and they believed in educating me alongside of the normal school curriculum. With that education came the understanding that we as black people were living in very dangerous times, but we held onto the hope of change coming, like that old Sam Cook song.

"Pop..."

"Just let me do the talking, Stephon," he replied, noticing, like I had, that there was an officer approaching on each side of the car.

After one last puff, he put his cigar in the ashtray and reached to open the glove compartment to grab his registration. What happened next transpired so fast that I didn't have time to utter a syllable from my mouth.

"He's reaching, he's reaching!" the cop on my side of the car screamed.

"Gun!"

His partner yelled back, and suddenly the summer evening was shattered with a roar of thunder so loud I thought God was screaming in my ear. But God wasn't screaming. God wasn't there. The liquid on my face and the weight on my shoulder told me what one thing was there in the moment with me. Death. And the screams were now my own.

CHAPTER TWO

"…And in local news, breaking overnight there was another fatal shooting of an unarmed black man in Ashburn, Virginia. Stephon Harris Sr., age fifty-three, was travelling on Clover Lane sometime yesterday evening when he was pulled over by two Loudon County police officers. At this time the details of what exactly transpired are unknown, but what should've been a routine traffic stop has ended in another senseless tragedy. We do know that Mr. Harris was travelling with his teenage son, and that nothing resembling a weapon was recovered at the scene. No one other than Mr. Harris was injured in the shooting. The Loudon County Police Department has yet to issue a statement, but we here at Channel Five News will keep you informed with up to the minute details. Sadly, this latest killing is one of many in recent months involving unprovoked violence towards African Americans at the hands of law enforcement. The shootings in Tulsa, Oklahoma and Charlotte, North Carolina were also…."

"Baby, you don't need to be watching this," she said, using the remote to silence the newscast.

I knew it was just her maternal instincts to protect me, but deep down she had to have known that we were beyond that. It didn't matter what was on T.V. because I'd lived that moment and it was something I'd never forget.

"I just don't understand, Mom. I mean he just shot him for no reason. It happened so fast that it didn't make sense, but even as I replay it in my mind, I still can't make sense of it."

"I know, sweetheart," she said, sitting beside me on the living room couch and taking my head in her lap.

I couldn't remember the last time I'd cried before all of this, but now it felt like I had enough tears to drown the world out. I didn't understand how my father, my best friend, and hero could be suddenly gone. I'd always known how fortunate I was to grow up in a two-parent household, especially given the fact that we were black. My understanding of just how rare that was made my relationship with my father that much more special to me. As long as I could remember, he'd always been there when I needed him, but now all I had left were memories and tears.

"It's not fair," I whispered in disbelief, closing my eyes on the tears as my mother gently stroked my head.

I could feel her own tears moistening my scalp, but still I felt a power exuding from her that told me she wouldn't break nor fold.

"No, it's not fair, Stephon. It's life. It's harsh and it's brutal and it's painful, but there's a plan that's bigger than what we can see in the moment. We..."

"Mom, please don't talk to me about God right now. I don't wanna be disrespectful or blasphemous, but I can't deal with a conversation on God's divine power and planning."

She gave me the silence I requested while still giving me all the love I needed. I'd heard the hollowed words of time healing wounds, but just as sure as I knew I'd lost a piece of myself, I knew time couldn't fix this. Growing up in D.C., while going to school in Virginia, had given me perspective on poverty and education, and on the history it carried with black people. In the late seventeen hundreds while Lynch gave a speech in Jamestown, Virginia on how to keep the black slaves in line, divided, and broken, and here it was two thousand and sixteen and a black man's life still held so little value. How was that possible? How had a white cop walked up on my father and shot him in cold blood?

I'd seen violence from a distance, but never had it invaded my space like this. Even lying there in the safety of my mother's arms I could still smell the gunpowder mixed with the remnants of cigar smoke. I could still feel my father's blood and brain matter heat up the skin on my face like I'd been burned. I just couldn't understand how shit had gotten to this point! I could remember months ago when Colin Kaepernick started the conversation about the inequalities in America by his refusal to participate in the national anthem. I remember other athletes supporting his message through different acts of protest and contributions to charities. I remember thinking that things were gonna change.

But change didn't happen fast enough to save my father's life, and now I was left wondering how a great man meant so little simply because of the color of his skin. Had it been a white man driving that Mercedes E class in that affluent neighborhood, he wouldn't have gotten a second glance, let alone been pulled over. But he wasn't white.

"I just keep thinking about how many conversations we had about the dangers of being a black man in America. I told my dad I understood, and I did, but I didn't get it. I didn't live through the civil rights movement or the Watts Riots, and you both did your best to keep me out of harm's way. You shielded me without sheltering me, but I still didn't get it. And now I wish I didn't understand. I wish my dad was still here, and it's my fault he's gone because he had to come pick me up and..."

"Shhh. Baby, you know your father wouldn't want you to carry the blame for any of this, and I won't hear of it either. No one knows when it's their time to go or how the Lord will call them home, but everyone knows death is a part of life. I had twenty-three wonderful years to share time and space with your father, and selfishly that will never be enough in my mind. I do think I know him well enough to know that he would never ever consider what happened to be your fault. That man loved you beyond measure and you know that. All he wanted was your happiness and we all know that Melody makes you happy."

"Yeah, but being in that neighborhood and being black...."

"Son, that neighborhood ain't to blame. How many Washington Redskin football players have houses out there? And you know the parties they throw, because I'm pretty sure you snuck into a few. What happened is solely because of the individual that pulled the trigger."

"So what happens now?" I asked, sitting up to face my mom.

She looked tired and worn, definitely older than her fifty years. But at the same time I saw the familiar look of decisive determination in her brown eyes. That same look had given me comfort to take out many obstacles, and in this moment it gave me hope to know I wasn't alone.

"I'm not sure what happens now, but we're gonna do what we gotta do."

"When are they gonna bring the cop up on charges?"

"First things first, we have to be at the police station at noon so you can give your statement. They wanted to do it last night, but the doctor and I both agreed that you needed to be sedated, given everything that happened. The lawyer's gonna meet us down there."

"The lawyer?"

"Yeah, you don't have a lot of experience in police stations, but when you walk in black you're automatically starting with two strikes against you. It's best to have a lawyer, just in case."

"If you say so, Mom. That means we have a little less than an hour, so I guess I should take a shower and get dressed."

"A shower? I thought you took one last night?"

I could feel my mouth open to respond to her question, but no words came out. How could I explain to her that I still felt every drop of my father's blood on my flesh? What words wouldn't sound horrible when trying to explain the way it seemed like my skin was crawling every few seconds? I didn't feel clean and I didn't know that I ever would again.

"It'll help wake me up," I replied lamely.

"Okay, I've got some things to take care of," she said, placing a kiss on my forehead before she got up off the couch.

The visible squaring of her shoulders was just another indicator of her strength, but I knew how strong she was. Grief wouldn't topple this woman, but still I would need to be strong and vigilant because all we had was each other. I got up and made my way down the hall, for once actually seeing our home, instead of simply passing through it. Even though I was an only child, my parents still thought four bedrooms and a basement was the proper space for us. It gave mom room to grade her school papers until she'd retired, and gave dad his man cave that allowed him to keep his sanity. I was given free reign, allowed to play wherever I desired, as long as it wasn't out in the streets, where so many of my peers would find the beginning to their end.

As I got older I sometimes resented the fact that I couldn't run the streets, but walking this familiar hallway with memories flooding my mind made me understand just how fortunate I was. I didn't try to stop the tears that were staining my cheeks, because in this moment they contained happiness. I needed that. Walking into my room, I grabbed my phone off my bed and saw that I had over thirty missed calls from Melody alone. I knew she was just wanting to make sure I was okay, but I didn't feel like talking. I grabbed everything I needed and spent the next thirty minutes scrubbing my brown skin until it had a reddish hue!

I knew cleansing myself of what happened was impossible, and trying to prolong having to relive those moments for a broken justice system only made me a coward. My father deserved justice and so I would have to tell his story. With my mind spinning in so many directions I didn't notice her when I first walked into my room, but then I did.

"What are you doing here?" I asked with my hand on the doorknob.

"Baby, your mom let me in, I'm s…so sorry. I know how much you loved your dad and how devastating this must be for you."

I believed her words, but still something kept me from going to her. My mind kept going back to the fact that I was at her house, and if I hadn't been there my dad would still be alive. So was I blaming her? I didn't want to answer that question, but I felt an anger building inside me the longer I looked at her tear-streaked face.

"I'm fine. You need to leave."

"Leave?" she questioned with surprise in her voice. "No, I don't wanna leave, baby. I wanna be here with you."

"I said I'm fine, Melody. I have to get dressed so my mom and I can go to the police station and give my statement."

"I'm so…so sorry, Steph…"

"Yeah, you said that already."

"Why are you being an asshole to me? I know you're hurting, but…"

"You don't know shit!" I yelled, frustrated.

"You didn't shoot your father. You don't have his blood on you or on your hands. His blood is not on your hands, Stephon. And I may not have lost my father, but I lost a man I loved and respected. I lost the man who gave me the greatest gift I've ever known, which is you. I lost my father-in-law," she whispered wiping the tears from her eyes.

Those eyes had never been so blue, and I'd never seen so much pain in them. Beneath that pain I saw love and I felt my anger evaporate as I closed the door and crossed the room to where she sat on my bed. Dropping to my knees, I placed my head against her neck, pulling her towards me, and I wept with uncontrollable sobs. I could feel her body shaking against my own and I knew she was tasting the salt of her tears as well. It was a good ten minutes before we were able to pull ourselves together, and when I looked in her eyes again, I found pure compassion. That added to my determination. In that moment, I could still hear the last conversation me and my father had, and I was so thankful I'd had his wisdom for that life changing discussion. Maybe one day when we were married I would share our talk with Melody, but for now I knew I had to embrace that moment.

"Melody, you know I love you, right?"

"Yes, baby, I know that."

"I'm sorry I lashed out at you earlier and I promise I won't try to shut you out anymore."

"It's okay, Stephon, I understand."

"Good because there's something I need to ask you."

"Anything, sweetheart, I'm here for you."

"Marry me," I said in a rush.

"Ma...marry you?" she replied obviously shocked.

While it was true I'd just mentioned this very thing to her yesterday, I know my timing was throwing her off.

"Yes, baby, I want you to marry me. I promise this is not a knee jerk reaction and it's not the grief talking either. One day I'll tell you about the long talk I had with my father regarding this very subject. For now, I need you to understand that I love you and I never see a moment in life without you right by my side. You've been my everything since we were twelve years old and you always will be. Marry me!"

The beautiful smile, through her fresh wave of tears, made my heart thump a little harder in my chest.

"Of course I'll marry you," she replied, pulling my face to hers and covering it with kisses.

To find joy on the heels of a moment filled with so much sorrow was almost impossible, but she was that for me, and I was smart enough to know the value in that.

"I'll get you a ring A.S.A.P. I promise..."

"Baby, as long as you say I'm yours that's all that matters. There will be time to take care of everything," she assured me.

"Stephon?" my mom called from right outside of my door.

"Come in, Mom," I said, standing and securing my towel around my waist. One look at my mother and I could tell more than the obvious was wrong.

"What is it, Mom, what happened?"

"We…we've gotta go. We gotta go to the police station now, because there's a problem."

"Problem, what problem?" I asked, feeling the taste of dread creep into the back of my throat.

"Th…the lawyer, he said there's a video of the shooting. He said it's gonna be your word against the cops."

I turned to Melody only to find a horrified look on her face, because we all understood what the lawyer was really saying. The cops were about to get away with killing my father because my word wouldn't count for shit against two white cops. Black lives were expendable, and I was just another nigger's son.

CHAPTER THREE

I tried using the ride to the police station to get my emotions under control, but the more I thought about the injustices of the past, the more worried I got. That worry gave way to anger, and it was justifiable considering how bloody the summer had been with police related shootings of black men. I wanted my father's death to be different. I needed it to be different, because if it wasn't then that meant he died for nothing. I couldn't even entertain that thought. Despite what the lawyer said, I was trying to keep an open mind and have some type of hope that there were still some decent cops around. Maybe I was being naïve, but that was better than being cynical.

"It'll work out," Melody whispered in my ear, squeezing my hand for reassurance.

I gave her the best smile I could before looking past her to see the protestors and reporters lined up across from the station. There were signs demanding justice for my dad and others that had died at the hands of cops. I wondered if people would riot if shit didn't turn out right, because it was obvious a lot were tired of being second-class citizens.

"Mom, where are we meeting the lawyer?"

"He said he'd be waiting for us at the front desk, when we walked in," she replied, pulling into a parking space between two cop cars.

Both cars were the same navy blue in color, and without any departmental decals, as the car that pulled us over. I felt a tightness in my chest and I felt something worse than panic coming on, causing my body to tremble.

"It's okay. I'm right here," Melody said, squeezing my hand tightly.

Seeing the calm in her eyes forced me to take deep breaths and summon the strength I knew the next few hours would require. It was too soon to take shit one day at a time, so it would have to be one hour at a time, or minute by minute, if necessary.

"Mom?"

She answered the question in my eyes with a slight nod of the head and I once again saw her square her shoulders. Opening the rear door behind the driver's side, I stepped out of my mom's escalade into the crisp winter afternoon, still holding Melody's hand as she followed. I opened my mom's door and helped her out, taking her hand in my free one and squeezing it in reassurance. We made the seemingly long walk into the police station in a three-wide line of unity, ignoring shouted questions from reporters, while accepting well-wishers support with silent nods. We may not have been a part of this community, but it was evident this community was behind us. That support added to our strength so that when we walked into the station it was battle readiness radiating from every pore in our bodies. As soon as we were through the door a slender built black man, about six foot one inch wearing an expensive suit, got up from the seat he'd been occupying by the desk and headed straight for us.

"Marlene, I'm sorry we have to meet again under these circumstances. And I'm so sorry for your loss."

"Thank you, Clark. You remember my son," she replied shaking his hand and turning towards me.

Clark Douglas was an old friend that my father had gone to school with at LSU and they'd stayed in touch, despite living on opposite coast. I hadn't seen him since our family vacation five years ago, but I was glad he'd flown out here immediately.

"Stephon, how you holding up?" he asked clasping my hand.

"I'm doing the best I can, Mr. Douglas. I'd be doing even better if you told me these muh'fuckas weren't about to get away with blatant cold blooded murder."

I saw him flinch slightly at the obvious anger in my voice before looking behind him to see who was eavesdropping. He guided us further away from the desk to a row of seats by the front door before he spoke again. We sat side by side with my mother and me on either side of him and Melody by my side holding my hand.

"Your father was one of my best friends and I want nothing more than to get justice for him. I know damn well he didn't have a weapon nor would he act like he did, especially with you in the car. I also know these cops are gonna try to spin this situation until it's justified, because they're scared of what the consequences of truth will bring. So, here's what I know so far. There is a dash cam video of the stop and you can see officers Chase McDaniels and Eric Hurley flanking the Mercedes. You can hear Officer Hurley yell your dad was reaching twice and you can hear Officer McDaniels holler "gun" before firing two shots through the driver side window. The problem is that somehow both officers body cams malfunctioned, so we can't see what they saw when they walked up on the car."

"That sounds awfully convenient," my mom said, disgusted.

"Indeed it does, but they've managed to produce work orders from other officers who complained about body cam malfunctions during routine traffic stops."

"Were any of the other people involved in those traffic stops hurt or killed?" I asked.

"No, they weren't, but..."

"Then I don't give a fuck. They shot my dad for no fucking reason. They didn't even have a reason to pull him over!"

"Their reason for that is that they were allegedly checking his well-being because he sat at a stop sign longer than necessary."

"We were just talking," I said, remembering the pause for conversation.

"I'm not disputing that, Stephon. I need you to tell me exactly what happened from the time you got in the car," he said.

I ran it all down to him in as much detail as I could remember up until the shooting started, because then everything got fuzzy.

"Okay, well the cop who fired the shots is saying he saw your dad leaning over reaching for what he thought was a gun, based on the warning his partner issued."

"And I'm telling you that's bullshit," I replied empathetically.

"There's the captain right there, so let's go and get this out of the way. I need you to listen to me in here, Stephon, because they're gonna try to trick you in any way they can. When I say, stop talking, stop talking, okay?"

"Okay," I said getting to my feet.

I kissed Melody and hugged my mom before following Mr. Douglas back into the depths of the precinct. We passed two interview rooms before we were ushered into one that was reminiscent in size to the prison cells I saw in movies. The air was thick with leftover smoke and bad breath from its previous occupants, and the battered wooden table with four chairs around it could definitely tell stories of its own. My first thought was that this setting had to have been chosen with thoughts of intimidation in mind. Here I was a privileged black kid who'd so far defied the odds by never knowing what the steel of handcuffs felt like on my wrists. Or in their minds, an uppity nigger.

I wasn't scared though, not in the slightest, because one of the many things my father taught me was that when you're right you've gotta stand on it without fear. I could admit I was stepping into a world not of my own design, but I didn't have a choice in the matter.

"Please have a seat, Mr. Harris, and let me say that I'm sorry for your loss."

His badge said Captain John Smith, but for a moment I had to bite my tongue because I was ready to call him everything except white Jesus.

"Th...thank you, Captain Smith."

"Now as you know you're not in any type of trouble, but I'm obligated to let you know that everything you say in these interview rooms is recorded per policy," he informed us.

"We understand, Captain, so let me state that I'm Attorney Clark Douglas and I'm here as both a friend and in my official capacity for the Harris family."

"Mr. Douglas, aren't you from the west coast?" the Captain asked with a polite smile that went nowhere near his eyes.

"I'm licensed to practice in D.C, Maryland and Virginia too, but we'll wait on this interview if you'd like to verify that."

"No, that's not necessary, the Chief-of-Police wants answers."

"As do we, so proceed, Captain."

"Okay. Mr. Harris, will you walk me through everything you remember."

I had to take a deep breath before I opened my mouth to speak, forcing down the bile that was rising in my throat.

"My dad came to pick me up from my fiancé's house, which is not far from where we got stopped. We were riding along having a conversation when the cops were suddenly behind us with their lights and sirens on."

"What was the nature of your conversation?" Captain Smith asked.

"I don't see what that has to do with anything," Mr. Douglas interjected quickly.

"Maybe they were arguing or plotting to do something nefarious..."

"Okay, make that the first and last time you treat my client like a suspect," Mr. Douglas said. I could feel my skull heating up with anger, but I did my damnedest to not let it show.

"Why were you two sitting at a stop sign at the corner of Clover and Rose?" Captain Smith asked, moving along seemingly unfazed.

"Because we were talking. Is it a crime to stop at a stop sign?"

"No, not at all, Mr. Harris, but that is what prompted the vehicle stop. Tell me what happened once the officers got behind you and your father."

"My dad pulled over and told me to let him do the talking, and..."

"Are you incapable of speaking for yourself for some reason, Mr. Harris?"

"Look Captain..."

"Hold on, Mr. Douglas, let me answer. No, Captain Smith, I'm very capable of speaking for myself as you can see, but my father was used to the treatment afforded black men who drive fancy cars in white neighborhoods," I replied with a knowing stare.

I caught the slight flush around his gray eyes and the lie he wanted to keep hidden about racial profiling. I put him at about late sixties early seventies in age, which meant his memory of how minorities were treated was probably rich with personal stories. He had a way of looking at me as if to say 'nigger you ain't shit,' but I wouldn't presume to know his inner most thoughts.

"What happened next, Mr. Harris?" he asked.

"My father put his cigar in the ashtray, and was getting ready to get his registration out when the cop on my side started yelling about him reaching. Then the other cop shouted gun and started shooting."

"Had anyone told your father to get his registration?"

"No."

"How do you know that was what he was going in the glove compartment for? Maybe he had something else in mind."

"Did you find anything else in the glove compartment besides his registration and insurance papers?" I challenged.

"We're still going over the vehicle at this time, sir. What happened after the shots were fired?"

"I...I don't know."

"What do you mean, Mr. Harris?"

"I mean I was in shock. Nothing made sense in the moment."

"So when did you have the presence of mind to pick up the gun?"

"*What?*"

"That's it, Captain, this interview is over," Mr. Douglas yelled outraged.

"Wait, what the fuck did you just say to me?" I demanded, standing up so fast that I flipped my chair over.

"I'm just asking the necessary questions, gentlemen, so..."

"No, you're just trying to cover your ass, muh'fucka, because you knew my dad didn't have no goddamn gun, or any other weapon! He was an honest black man who never had so much as a parking ticket and your cracker cop friend gunned him down for no reason!"

"That's enough, Stephon..."

"It ain't enough and it ain't alright! I'm telling you right now, Captain, that you better not try to sweep this under the rug or try to make me or my father out to have done something wrong. You better stand for justice!"

"I better? Or what, Mr. Harris, what exactly are you saying?" Captain Smith asked smirking in defiance.

"Stephon enough!" Mr. Douglas warned, turning me to face him and giving me a much-needed moment to bite my tongue before I said something I couldn't take back.

"Let's go, this interview is over," he said, taking my hand and leading me from the room like a scolded child. I wanted to stick my size twelve Jordan in the Captain's ass, but getting locked up for assault wouldn't help anyone.

"What's wrong? What happened?" my mother asked, immediately noticing the look on my face and how eager Mr. Douglas was to get us out of there.

"Just cops being cops, Marlene, come on let's get out of here," he replied, ushering all of us out the doors.

"Baby, are you okay?" Melody asked, catching my hand as we walked towards the car.

I wanted to scream at the top of my lungs so the world would understand how not okay I was. I should've been working towards grieving for my father, but here I was having to listen to insulting questions in the backyard of fucking Mayberry! It was obvious the cops didn't want the truth to come out, but I'd be damned if I let them use me to bury it. Tightening my grip on Melody's hand, I made an abrupt detour in the opposite direction of my mom's truck and made a beeline for the still building crowd across the street. I could hear my mom and Mr. Douglas calling my name, but I ignored them and headed for the closest T.V. crew and camera. A hush descended when we got up on the crowd. I may have been too young to participate in the civil rights movement or the many marches for freedom, but in this moment I knew what injustice felt like, it was in the spirit of Malcolm, Martin, and Mandela that drove me to speak out against this injustice.

"My father was a good man, a decent and hardworking man who went out of his way to help others. He wasn't violent, he didn't party or drink, and he stayed married to the same woman for twenty-three years without ever cheating. No one is perfect and I get that, but my father didn't deserve to be slaughtered with-

out cause. I just spent thirty minutes inside the police station behind me being questioned by Captain Smith, who asked me
things like why did my dad stop at a stop sign and what did I do
with the gun.

"There was no gun, my father never owned a gun, because
he trusted in the laws and police to protect him. Now those same
police want to justify shooting an unarmed black man driving a
sixty thousand dollar car while in a white neighborhood! There
is no justification! Conveniently, the police officer's body cams
malfunctioned, so you can't see what they saw inside the car, but
I was there. I was inside that car when that officer scattered my
father's brains onto my face. The shooting was unprovoked and
I demand justice, not just for my father and my family, but for
everyone who has lost a loved one to senseless gun violence.
Give us all justice…or learn to live without peace."

ASAD

CHAPTER FOUR

Three Days Later

It seemed like the statement I gave after my police interview had set the world on fire. Protests had broken out all across the country, some peaceful and others that resulted in people losing their lives. I wasn't sure how I felt about that. I was truly numb at this point and unsure of what my next move should be. My Instagram followers had jumped into the millions overnight, filled with both regular people and famous people reaching out to me with wishes of condolences, hope, and strength. As angry as I was, I didn't wanna be the cause of continuous rioting, so I used my following to introduce the world to the man I lost.

I posted old photos and home movies, sometimes I just shared stories about things my dad and I had done together. It helped me in some way to know there were people out in the world listening, or even relating, to all I'd lost. For every good there's a bad though, because I got countless questions and insensitive comments about the 'white girl' I was seen holding hands with. It was crazy to me how people could be so ugly or narrow-minded for no reason, but I wouldn't let that shake the love I had for my woman.

It only took a day for Melody to pull a Lebron James and go zero dark thirty on all social media, and even though I didn't want her to hide herself from the world, I still respected her decision. I refused to back down though, even going so far as to post something on my Instagram page that showed a picture of an interracial couple and it said every black king needs a white queen. I got a lot of backlash for that, but those who understood the chess metaphor as it pertains to life liked the picture and caption. I should have expected the backlash, especially from black women, 'cause of the way a lot of black men use white women as a symbolism of success or having 'made it.' I wasn't on that though. I love all women equally, because I understood without them there was no me. In this moment I had to defend my woman and our relationship. I couldn't please everybody, but none of this was about that or me. It was about the value of all black lives, because it seemed like the world didn't care as long as it was our blood being spilled.

My meeting with the District Attorney had gone better than the one with Captain Smith, but there was still no word on there being a prosecution. I was getting impatient, but I tried not to let it show for my mother's sake. Melody and I had done as much as possible to help her with the funeral arrangements, and I'd even done the impossible thing of getting my dad's car from the police lot. It took everything in me not to completely lose it just at the sight of the car, so instead of driving it, I had it towed to the nearest auto body shop that did upholstery. My mom and I hadn't decided on whether or not to sell the car, but that was a decision to make for a later date.

I was doing my best to run the business from home and Melody had actually been spending time in training on site at the store in order to do my old job. We didn't just sell paint we actually did a lot of interior design for homes and offices, and thankfully, Melody was natural in that department. We were young and hadn't gotten our degrees yet, but our staff was seasoned and longtime customers remembered my father training me on the business as I grew up, so our business wasn't suffering. My mom was in no state of mind to run the company, so we stepped up in her absence. No one was working today though. Today we would all gather and pay our respects to my father in a small, yet beautiful, service. I guess as a sign of maturity, my parents had made a lot of the arrangements and picked out their burial arrangements ahead of time.

Had I known this earlier in life, it would've disturbed me, but for now I was grateful not to have all that stress and burden on my mom. I knew she cried a lot when she was behind closed doors, but out in the open she was the embodiment of strength. When I looked at her I tried to imagine how I would feel if I lost Melody in a sudden violent manner. I couldn't do it, I loved her too much to think about letting her go, and so I had no idea how my mother remained upright. I'd do anything to see her stay that way though, which was why I was at this very moment making sure all the last-minute details were tended to.

We only had about two hours before the service started, but the first Baptist church was only a couple of miles away in the northeast section of D.C. I peeked in on my mom to make sure she was getting the nap I insisted she take, because I knew the day would be emotionally exhausting. My plan now was to take a quick shower, get dressed, and get something to eat, but all that changed when I stepped into the room to find Melody quietly crying. She'd more or less moved in and been by my side, so seeing her wasn't a surprise, but to find her crying was. Her back was to me, but still I heard the sniffles and saw her shoulders shaking.

"What is it, baby?" I asked, closing the door and crossing the room to sit next to her on my bed.

"Nothing, I'm fine," she replied, wiping her face quickly and putting her phone on the nightstand.

"It's obviously something, because you've been crying. Talk to me."

"I'm okay, Stephon, I'm gonna go check on your mom."

"I just did that," I said, pulling her onto my lap to stop her from fleeing.

I knew she didn't want to burden me with whatever was on her mind, but it was important for her to understand that I was her support system just like she was mine. Wiping away the remaining tears from her cheeks, I held her close and waited for her to get herself under control.

"It's nothing, baby, just stupid people on social media saying shit," she finally said.

"Saying shit like what?" I snapped.

"The usual mean things that bullies say. That I'm fat and ugly."

"And you know that's complete bullshit, right?"

"I know you think so, but..."

"Baby, don't. You know that you're an absolutely gorgeous woman, regardless of what me or anyone else thinks. Don't let anyone steal your self-confidence or your joy, because you've fought too hard against body issues to go backwards now."

"I know, babe, but it's not just that...pe...people are calling me a nigger lover and a black man's whore. I mean it's 2016, so why are mixed couples still a topic of discussion?"

"Because there's still ignorance in the world, sweetheart. People are angry right now because the inequalities imposed on black people have barely changed in sixty years, and they're tired of it. It's understandable, but we can't let that affect what it is we have and what we built. We don't owe anyone an explanation of our love, and we definitely don't need to be ashamed of it. Don't let other people's ignorance define your life, okay?"

"I won't, baby. As long as I know you're right here with me I'll always fight for this amazing love we have," she replied kissing me softly.

Sometimes words just aren't enough and you have to be defined by your actions. With this in mind, I took our kisses from those of comfort to the levels of full-blown passion that words tend to complicate. The only interruption came when I pulled her t-shirt off and laid her gently across my bed. No matter how many times I saw her through these eyes, she was always stunningly beautiful and my hunger for her was immediate. It only took seconds for me to shed my own sweats and t-shirt before slowly, and seductively, removing her panties. My lips heated her flesh as I kissed up her leg to her thigh, and over to her other thigh in an effort to give equal attention.

I could feel her heartbeat thumping in that most secret of places when I put my lips to hers, and I thrilled in the way her body responded as I began my feast. She tasted better than a home-cooked meal, and her appreciation for my appetite was more than evident in the screams she was fighting to muffle.

"Shhh, you're gonna wake my mom," I whispered smiling up at her.

"I...I can't, it's your fault," she panted, grabbing two fistfuls of sheets when I locked in on the little man in the boat.

When I felt the shaking start in her toes I knew it was time to take it to the next level. The way we fit together made it amazing every time, but in this moment, I needed her to know that it was about more than sex.

"I love you, Melody," I said, setting a slow rhythm of powerful strokes in an effort to drive my point home.

"I lo...love you to...too, baby," she replied, holding onto me tightly.

The sounds of our passion were trapped in between our kisses, but as the fires raged inside both of us the pleasure became undeniable. Without warning we found ourselves above the clouds and I watched the look of shock on her face when we kicked down the doors of heaven.

"You...you...but why?" she asked.

"What do you mean?" I replied, rolling off her, yet pulling her close to me.

"I mean we've been together a long time, and we've had a lot of sex, but you've never cum inside me without a condom on. Why now?"

"Because we didn't just have sex, baby, we made love. I'm in love with you, Melody, and whatever comes with that I'm with it."

The tears I saw in her eyes now were accompanied by a smile that touched my heart. This was the woman I was gonna spend the rest of my life with and I wasn't about to let nothing or no one make her feel inferior.

"Pass me your phone, babe."

She gave me a puzzled look, but did as I asked. Once I made sure I had her secured by my side underneath the covers I logged into her Facebook page and went to Instagram so we could make a video.

"Stephon, what are you doing?"

"Just trust me, you know I got you," I assured her, giving her a quick kiss and pushing her brown hair out of her eyes. Holding the phone up to make sure we could be seen I hit the record button.

"Love is a lot of things, but it's never something to be ashamed of. If you don't like us, or our relationship, we really don't care, just know that we're not ashamed of it and we damn sure won't let you dictate it. Live your life like we live ours... with no regrets." I stopped the recording there and went about posting it for the world to see.

"Why'd you do that?"

"Because I love you, and because anyone who comes after you is coming after me. We're in this together, sweetheart, and I pray I have as many years with you as my parents had together."

"Me too," she replied kissing me again.

I loved her smile. With everything that had happened, it felt good to see a genuine smile, because they were few and far between. As much as we both would've like to bask in our afterglow, I knew there was still a lot to do and a long way to go before the day was over. We showered together before dressing in our respective black outfits. Putting on my black suit brought back the memory of me and my dad going to get ours tailored together. He felt that as a grown man one needed a nice suit and a black one would get you through any occasion.

I would wear mine on this day out of love and respect, and he would be buried in his. After I was dressed I made my mom a cup of coffee and took it to her, knowing she would need her energy as much as my support. Once she was dressed and ready we left for the church. When we got there, Melody and I welcomed everyone while my mom spent some time alone with her husband. I didn't know if I'd have the strength to say goodbye, I didn't even know how to formulate the words.

When my mom came out and gave me the signal that it was my turn, I could've sworn that I heard my knees rattling harder than the man in the *Wizard of Oz*. The walk into the back of the church was the longest of my life, but when I finally made it back there I was relieved at how peaceful he looked. The mortician had done a damn good job with the bullet wound, which meant we could have an open casket. I still couldn't find the words though. I mean, it seemed surreal that my father, of all people, would be dead like this. I didn't wanna question God, but how could this be right? How was this innocent life snuffed out so easily and so early? I didn't have the answers, but I'd never stop searching for them.

"We'll get justice, Pops. I promise," I said, bending down to kiss his forehead before turning to leave.

On my way back into the main sanctuary of the church, I saw that the doors were all the way open, which meant the casket would be rolled in soon and the service would begin. Several news crews had wanted to be allowed inside, but I made it clear really quickly that this wasn't some spectacle. Any disrespect on this day would get somebody fucked up without hesitation. I was making my way back towards the front of the church where Melody was when my peripheral vision caught my mother collapsing into Mr. Douglas' arms. The panic I felt couldn't be described, but thankfully my feet were moving of their own accord.

"Mom! Mom, are you alright?" I asked, grabbing her hand.

Her tears were too powerful for her to answer through. She was almost choking on each sob. I looked at Mr. Douglas for answers and the knots in my stomach tightened as I looked into his face.

"The district attorney said there's not enough evidence to charge the officer and convict. I'm sorry, there's nothing I can do about it."

CHAPTER FIVE

February 2017

"Baby, I figured you wouldn't want to go out or do anything special for Valentine's Day, so I decided to cook for us," Melody informed me when she walked into our room and began changing from her work outfit.

Despite my arguments and reasoning months ago we now lived together in the house I'd grown up in. I hadn't wanted to leave my mom, and Melody felt the same way about me, so here we were. I was grateful, even if I wasn't great at showing it. I spent a lot of time in the same position I was now, which was flat on my back staring at the ceiling in search of answers that wouldn't come. I found myself needing more and more time alone with my thoughts, which was why I was grateful that Melody was here to make sure my mom was all right.

It wasn't like she needed a babysitter or anything, I just knew I wasn't worth a fuck the last two months. Luckily, I was able to work on autopilot, and thank God Melody was a natural or the company would've gone under. I found it hard to really be motivated about anything when nothing in life made sense to me anymore. There wasn't a day that passed where I didn't question why my dad wasn't here with us, but I still had no answer for that. To make matters worse, tomorrow was his birthday.

I knew that was the real reason Melody was giving me a pass in the Valentine's Day festivities, but she didn't have to, because I'd come to terms with a solution that would give me peace. It was the contemplation of this solution that had me lying in bed staring at the ceiling, but I wasn't looking for answers as much as I was a sign that I'd actually lost my damn mind. After looking at my decision from various angles I came to the conclusion that even if I had lost my mind, so what. I am what they made me.

"What are you thinking about cooking, babe?" I asked.

"I was kinda in the mood for some smothered pork chops over white rice, maybe some greens on the side."

"Sounds like a plan."

"Glad you approve. I invited Mom, but she said she'd rather spend Valentine's Day alone. What do you think about that?"

"I think we should respect her wishes. It's her first Valentine's Day and birthday without him, and she has to deal with that in her own way. Just like we have to."

"I just want a quiet evening with you, babe," she said slipping into some shorts and pulling one of my t-shirts on.

"I'm good with that. I did manage to get you a little something though," I told her, reaching into my pocket as I moved to stand in front of her.

Her gaze was quizzical because we both knew I was the worst at keeping any surprise for her a secret, but in this case, it was absolutely necessary. The look on her face when I pulled the box from my pocket and opened it to display the three-karat diamond ring I got her was worth every minute of secrecy. I'd worked alongside my dad in the family business most of my life. He always rewarded me for my efforts monetarily. I'd never been one who did what most teenagers dis, so as I got older I spent summers and school breaks working. My parents provided well for me, so I was able to save just about everything that I earned. I'd had to work long and hard to save the money to get this ring, but all the sweat and long hours I put in for the company were worth the smile on her face.

"Oh my god! Stephon, you didn't!"

"Yes I did, and it's long overdue."

She jumped into my arms, covering my face with noisy kisses before I even had the chance to put the ring on her finger. I knew she was genuinely surprised because I hadn't mentioned our wedding or engagement since I'd proposed. It never seemed like the right time. After we all absorbed the truth about the D.A. not bringing charges against the police for killing my father, no one really knew what to do. The masses rioted and protested in a show of support, but that didn't give us back what we lost, nor was there any sense of justice.

The message I took away from the whole situation was that the murder of black people was legal, but that still didn't help me sleep at night. Melody did help though. When the nightmares came, she held me without judgment. When the anger threatened to consume me, she was right there to talk me through it. And when the hate became part of my every breath, she continued to love me unconditionally. That was why it was important to me to show her that she still had my heart.

"I can't believe you did this, baby. Thank you, thank you, thank you!" she said, kissing me again and then backing up so I could put the ring on her finger.

"I gotta show Mom," she said laughing as she ran from the room.

I had no idea whether my mom knew of our engagement or not, since I never got into their womanly discussions, but I knew she loved Melody. Knowing my mom, she'd be relieved I wasn't like most dudes my age who had two or three kids by the same number of women, and couldn't take care of nobody. I learned from the best though and one good woman was enough for me.

"It's so beautiful!" Melody squealed coming back into the room, damn near tackling me.

"I'm glad you like it, babe." I said laughing at her excitement.

"Like it? I fucking love it! I already sent a picture of it to my mom and dad, and they send their congratulations. Oh, and my dad said you and him need to have a sit down."

The smile on her face as she delivered this news was down-right devilish, but I had expected her father would want to have a coming to Jesus talk. As an only child myself I knew what over-protectiveness looked like.

"I'll call him myself, but tonight my focus is on you, Mrs. Harris."

"Whatever you say, Mr. Harris. I'm going to start dinner."

"I'll help you," I offered, lacing my fingers through hers as we made our way to the kitchen.

My mom was an excellent cook, so she took pride in her kitchen, and made sure every state of the art cooking utensil was on standby. For the first time in a long time the mood was light and celebratory, and when I put on some music it turned into our very own private party. We put together an amazing meal, which we topped off with a treat of red wine my mom insisted we use to christen our engagement. After dinner, I ran Melody a hot bubble bath for the two of us and we bathed each other until the sexual tension had us running for the bedroom.

By candlelight we made love into the early morning hours and then I held her until she fell asleep with a smile on her face. As she slept, I laid there counting the minutes until an hour had passed. It was only when I was sure she wouldn't stir that I decided it was time to make my move. Making sure to move with as little noise as possible, I slipped from the bed and went to my closet where I grabbed an all-black sweat suit. Once I was dressed, I threw on my all black Reebok classics and tiptoed out the room, down the hall, and after turning off the alarm, I was out the back door. I had to take a minute and let my eyes adjust to the night before I stepped away from the back door and into the alley that ran behind my house.

Years of sneaking out had prepared me for this moment, so I knew to walk with purpose and like I belonged right where I was. The streets of D.C. never slept, which meant eyes and ears were always lurking, but that didn't faze me. Two blocks from my house was the all black Crown Victoria I'd bought a couple weeks back. Once I made sure everything I needed was in the duffle bag under the seat I was on my way. My journey was mapped out methodically and I'd probably done more dry runs than an Islamic Terrorist. I was still nervous though. I had no illusions of being a hood nigga, because that wasn't how I was raised, but I wasn't no bitch either.

In my opinion, the problem with most criminals was that they didn't really think their situation through and plan for shit to go wrong. Shit always went wrong and you couldn't plan for everything, but you could minimize your mistakes. I was on my way to put this theory to the test. It took concerted effort to quiet the screaming in my mind, because my conscience was more than uneasy with my decision, but there was no going back. I reached my destination a little before four a.m., which meant I didn't have time to waste because the sun would be up soon. One deep breath was all I took before I pulled my ski mask out of the bag and put it on.

I made sure my 9 mm Beretta was loaded and the silencer was screwed on tight. The only thing left to do was talk myself out of what I was about to do, but in my heart, I knew I was way beyond that. I'd parked at the end of the street, which meant I had to walk down into the cul-de-sac since the house I wanted was tucked in the corner. I could feel my heart beating in my throat as I scanned the house on both sides of the street searching for movement. As crazy as it sounded I was relying on my instincts to give me that feeling of somebody watching me, because I was in no way experienced in this type of cloak and dagger shit.

I made it to the back of the house and I immediately saw that my luck was still going strong because the basement was occupied by the one person I expected it to be. All people were creatures of habit and when you had a daily routine it was hard to stray from that. This man's crutch was his mandatory workout before work. It amazed me how those who viewed themselves as untouchable paid so little attention to the world around them, and who was watching them. About ten-feet from the back of this three-story townhouse was a path used by joggers and bike riders, and I knew it would only be minutes before he was out to run.

Despite how much I had planned this was the part I was uncertain about. I wanted to approach him as soon as he came out, but then I was running the risk of an early rising neighbor peeking out the window at us. My second option was to catch him on the path, but it was a guarantee that someone would see us at some point. I had to minimize the odds of witnesses. I was still contemplating my best move when I heard the back door slide open and the sound of footsteps crunching the frost-covered grass. Submerging myself in the shadows at the edge of the backyard, I waited and watched while he stretched and headed in my direction.

"Stop moving," I said when he was only a few feet away.

I knew he couldn't see my face or probably make out more than my body shape, but there was no mistaking the pistol in my out-stretched hands.

"Just take it easy. You don't wanna do anything stupid, I'm a..."

"I know exactly who you are, Officer McDaniels. You're smart enough to know this ain't some random occurrence."

"What do you want?" he asked warily.

"I want justice. Will you give me that?"

"I don't know what you mean."

"Two months ago you shot an unarmed black man, killing him for no reason."

"He had a gun..."

"Shut the fuck up with your lies!" I demanded in a fierce whisper, flipping the safety of the gun.

"Listen, mister, you weren't there, so you don't know..."

"But I was there. I know he didn't have a gun, that there never was a gun in the car. I know you shot him down in cold blood, just like I know if you don't want me to do the same to you, you're gonna make it right." I said, stepping closer to him.

"How?"

"You're gonna make a recording of yourself saying that you shot Mr. Harris and that he was unarmed. You're gonna tell the truth of why you did what you did and then you're gonna face the consequences."

"Okay, whatever you say. We can do it now if you want to, just take me where you want to go before my wife gets up."

"Don't worry I have no interest in hurting your wife or kids so…"

My ears came alert like a bloodhound as the sound of sneakers striking pavement grew louder in a hurry. Someone was coming and one look at him told me he was hearing it too, because I could just make out his smirk in the darkness. Even when I'd been planning for shit that could go wrong I'd thought I would have more time at this stage of the plan. If I just disappeared into the night without him I'd never get the chance again.

"Come on, let's go," I said.

"I don't think so, son. I know who you are and I know you ain't no killer, so unless you wanna get caught with your gun on a cop you better disappear."

I opened my mouth to argue, but the footsteps were getting louder along with the sound of my heartbeat in my ears. I had a moment of indecision, but in that moment clarity hit with the brilliance of lightening. The pistol jumped in my hand as the barrel coughed twice, and then his face disappeared. In a split second everything screamed run and that's exactly what I did. With the gun concealed under my sweatshirt I forced myself to jog at what I hoped was a normal rate to anyone who may have been watching.

Within moments I reached my car and I was behind the wheel trying not to leave rubber all over the street as I got the hell out of dodge. It took a few minutes before I remembered to pull the sweat-drenched mask off of my face, but it was still a work in progress to breath and not pass out. I couldn't afford a car accident. I just needed to maintain my composure and get out of Virginia without anyone knowing I'd been here. It still wasn't registering what I'd done, but I knew one thing for sure. There was no going back now…but truthfully, I didn't want to.

CHAPTER SIX

By the time the sun rose over the city I was back in the safety of my own bedroom, watching my woman sleep and asking myself how even the simplest things would be the same. I felt different. I didn't know if Melody would be able to notice any difference in me when she woke up, but I knew I'd changed. It didn't matter what my intentions were, I'd taken another man's life. I kept asking myself how I felt about that, because I knew there should be a whirlwind of emotions battling for dominance.

But the truth was I felt nothing. Officer Chase McDaniels didn't deserve my remorse, because he had none for my father or my family. He reaped what he sowed. The question now was what did I do next? The gun I'd used was already swimming at the bottom of the Potomac and my clothes had been burned. I didn't think suspicion would automatically be cast my way, but just in case I'd covered my ass. That still didn't answer the question of what's next.

"You know that watching me sleep is weird, right?" she asked, yawning loudly.

"It's not weird, baby, you're peaceful and beautiful when you sleep."

"Yeah and so are dead people. But you don't sit there and stare at them," she replied laughing.

For a second I thought she saw right through me and she'd known what I'd done, but the love I saw when I looked in her eyes eased my fears.

"Exactly how long have you been watching me anyway?"

"Not long. I was tempted to wake you up a few times though."

"Oh yeah, and why would you do that?" she asked, pulling me toward her until our lips met.

"Why do you think?"

"I don't know, why don't you show me," she suggested, tugging at my boxers until I got up and slid them off. I climbed under the covers and on top of her naked body, giving her a proper kiss to match my intentions.

"Mm, I love it when you wake me up like this," she sighed.

"Really? Show me how much you love it."

Accepting my challenge, she rolled me on my back and was on top of me with me buried deep inside her before I could catch my breath.

"Any questions?"

"Not one," I said, grabbing her hips as she slowly rose and fell.

"Stephon, are you up?" my mom called from right outside my door.

"Gi...give me a minute, Mom."

"Stephon, it's important, we gotta talk," she insisted.

I knew the doorknob would be turning momentarily and the smile on Melody's face was only making it harder to stop what we'd just started.

"I'm not done with you," I informed her.

"I'll hold you to that," she replied, laying down next to me and pulling the covers up to her chin.

"Come in, Mom," I called out.

She was already fully dressed with a cup of coffee in her hand that she extended to me before sitting on the edge of the bed.

"Something's happened," she said slowly.

I could feel a sudden heat in the back of my throat, but I used the warm coffee to fight down whatever was trying to come up.

"What is it, Mom?" Melody asked.

"All I know is that the cop who killed my husband was found in his backyard around five a.m. with two bullet holes in his face. The news just started running the report, but Clark called me earlier."

"Why did Mr. Douglas call you, Mom?" I asked calmly, even though I knew the answer.

"Well, because the cop who killed my husband turning up dead is gonna bring up questions for his family, and Clark doesn't want any of us to say anything without him."

"Is he coming back out here?" Melody asked.

"Only if he has to, but since I know no one in this house had anything to do with what happened to that cop then probably not," she replied.

I felt the intensity of my mother's stare as she made this statement, but I didn't let it cause unnecessary paranoia. If I thought the truth about what I'd done was lurking around every corner, I'd be jumping out of my damn skin by next week.

"What else do they know?" I asked.

"Apparently, he was out for his morning run, but he didn't make it off his property. His poor wife saw him lying there when she opened her blinds this morning, but they hadn't found any witnesses, a weapon, or a clear motive yet."

"I'm sure a crooked cop had a lot of enemies," Melody said seriously.

"You're probably right. Is it wrong that I don't feel bad? I mean, I admit I wanted to see him go to prison and suffer for what he'd done to my Stephon, but the Christian in me wouldn't allow me to wish him death. I'm not sorry he's gone though."

"Mom, it's your right to feel whatever you want to feel, no one can take that from you. You didn't owe that cop shit, okay?" I said.

"Yeah, I guess you're right. I do feel bad for his family, I know how that loss feels," she replied, standing up and heading for the door.

"You gonna be alright, Mom?" Melody asked.

"Yeah, sweetheart, I'm sorry I interrupted your morning sex…"

"Mom!" Melody exclaimed, blushing a deep red all over her face.

"What, it's not my fault you can smell it in the air," she replied laughing.

"That's so embarrassing! After I take a shower I'm gonna come see you for a little woman to woman chat," Melody said.

"Okay, sweetheart," my mom replied, still laughing as she closed the door behind her.

"Wow," I said, laughing to myself and putting the coffee cup on the nightstand.

"Indeed. You gotta love her though, and at least it wasn't my mom."

"True."

"Come on, babe, take a shower with me. It'll save time so we're not too late for work," Melody said.

"You don't wanna finish what you started?" I asked reaching for her.

"I've got something else in mind," she replied, dodging me and hopping out the bed to get what she needed for a shower.

I followed her lead, trying to put the conversation with my mom out of my mind and focus on making my woman happy.

"You gonna wash my back, babe?" I asked.

"Maybe if you play your cards right."

"Hmm, what's that mean exactly?"

"Get in here and I'll explain," she replied, pulling the shower curtains back to let me in.

I leaned in to kiss her, but she adverted her head and pulled my head towards her until her lips were right up against my ear.

"Where were you last night?" she asked. I tried to pull back, but she held me in place.

"I brought you in here because they can't hear us over the shower in case they're already listening. Don't bother to lie to me because when I got up at three-thirty in the morning to pee you weren't in the bed. You weren't even in the house. Where were you?"

This time she did release me from her grip. It took everything in me to keep a straight face as I searched her face for some sign that she was joking. She wasn't. Our relationship wasn't built on lies, but this was a completely different situation and I had a decision to make. I opened my mouth to speak, only to have the air forced from my lungs when she grabbed my dick roughly.

"Don't lie to me, Stephon."

"I was handling some business," I replied vaguely, hoping she valued what was in her hand as much as I did.

"Handling business, huh? I tell you what. I'm gonna prove to you that I've got your back no matter what. Hurry up and wash your ass," she ordered, letting me go and bathing herself.

I knew better than to try some frisky shit right now, so I simply followed her lead and did like I was told. I didn't know what she had planned or what she had on her mind, but I know what she thought she knew. I had no idea what to do about it though. I mean I trusted her, but this was fucking murder we were talking about. That was something you trusted no one with except maybe the dead man or woman. What were my options? Because it wasn't like I was gonna kill Melody. I reached for her and she didn't pull away from me, and when I kissed her I felt the same passion I always did. I was more confused than ever now!

"I love you, but no loving for you until later. Now come on," she said, turning the water off and leading the way out of the shower into our room.

"Get dressed, and put your black suit on," she ordered.

"My suit?"

"No time for questions. Just do it please."

There was pure determination in her eyes, but it wasn't as intimidating as it was sexy. There was obviously no point in arguing with her and I knew that from years of experience with her getting her way. I did as I was told while she disappeared to have whatever secret conversation she'd promised my mom. I didn't think she'd reveal to my mom that I hadn't been in the house all night just because I knew she wouldn't want to worry her. My mom wasn't stupid by a long shot, so she would put two and two together if the math was laid out in front of her. I damn sure wasn't prepared to deal with that, which meant I had to make sure Melody knew mum was the word.

"Okay, we're all set," Melody said coming back into the room and heading for the closet.

"All set for what?"

"Be patient, sweetheart, and you'll see."

"Is there a reason I'm wearing my black suit instead of a blue or grey one?"

"Black is traditional," she replied with a sly smile as she pulled out one of her white summer dresses.

"Baby, I don't think it's warm enough outside for that."

"Well then it'll be your job to keep me warm on our travels."

"Travels?"

"That's enough questions, now go downstairs and wait with your mom."

"Yes ma'am," I replied giving a mock salute as I slipped on my black loafers and headed out the door. I found my mom at the kitchen table nursing a cup of coffee and staring off into space.

"What is she up to?" I asked.

"That's your woman, and you know how determined she is when she sets her mind to something. I don't know what you did to prompt this next move, but there's no talking her out of it and you should probably get used to that."

"Do women always have to have their way?" I asked sitting at the table next to her.

"Son, there's been a saying around for many, many years. Happy wife, happy life. I promise you that you'll have more good days than bad if you live everyday like it's your last."

Her words carried with them a pain she couldn't stop from showing up on her face, and it made me reach for her hand. There was no doubt in my mind who she was thinking about, whose face she was seeing in every corner of her memory. I knew nothing I did could erase that pain, but at least now she knew the person responsible for her pain was dealt with.

"Let's get this show on the road," Melody said joining us in the kitchen.

Her transformation was so startling that my tongue was stuck to the roof of my mouth. Her summer dress came with matching heels, a little blush and some bright red lipstick that made those blue eyes sparkle like the ocean. Her mass of brown curls was piled high in a ponytail on top of her head with two delicate pieces framing her smiling face.

"Damn," I murmured, wishing we were headed back upstairs.

"I'll take that as a compliment. Now let's go."

"Where are we going?" I asked.

"Well, my darling fiancé, we're going to the courthouse to get our marriage license, and then we're going to get married."

"Say what?"

"You heard me, sweetheart. Now move your ass."

I looked at my mom and she gave me a smile that said 'remember what I told you.'

"Are you sure?" I asked Melody, standing and going to her so I could look into her eyes.

Whether we'd discussed it or not I knew *she knew* I had something to do with that cop being killed, but instead of judging me or being afraid of me, she was ready to promise forever. Who does that? In all the years we'd been together I hadn't underestimated her commitment to me, but knowing what this gesture meant at this time spoke volumes I never thought of.

"I'm sure," she replied taking both of my hands in her own, looking me directly in the eyes.

"Okay. Let's do this," I said smiling and pulling her into my arms.

I caught the smile on my mother's face as we walked out of the house and piled into her truck, and it was good to see. Despite all we'd lost, today would be a happy day. I wish my father could have been there for that moment, but to have his birthday and my wedding day coincide seemed poetic. On the ride to the courthouse I offered my help with making this day go off without issues, but I was informed that I'd be leaving everything in the capable hands of my soon-to-be wife.

I had my doubts, but I shouldn't have because we got the marriage license in record time and before I knew it we were standing face to face in the same church where we'd said goodbye to my father. Surprisingly, her mother and father were already there. She got the joy of having her dad walk her down the aisle, which put tears in both of our eyes. When my mom stood up for me in the form of a best man and handed me the ring I'd bought Melody, along with my dad's wedding band, I lost my battle to hold the tears in.

The emotion within both of us overflowed as we exchanged vows, but truer words had never been spoken before than when we both said, "I do." Looking at my wife I knew I had a partner and soul mate in every way that God had intended. I knew my father was smiling down on us and that he approved of all we had, and all we planned to build.

"You're amazing, babe. I can't believe you pulled this together so quickly," I told her as we danced our first dance in the parking lot of the church.

Thankfully, the system in my mom's Escalade was bumpin,' and she kept the classics on deck, so we we're dancing to K-Ci and JoJo's *All my Life*.

"I was determined, sweetheart, because this had to be done A.S.A.P."

"Oh yea, why's that?" I asked.

"Because a wife can't testify against her husband," she whispered in my ear.

"Baby, I…"

"No lies between us, Stephon, that and cheating are my deal breakers and you know that."

At first, all I could do was look at her because she was right, and I'd known how she was from the very beginning. But I loved her.

"You're right. I shot him, babe, and I'm not sorry."

"Tell me everything."

ASAD

CHAPTER SEVEN

Two Weeks Later

If I was worried about how my wife would react to me should the truth come out, I shouldn't have been. She wasn't a killer and didn't really have a mean bone in her body, but she was the type who believed anyone could kill when provoked with the right reason. She understood how much my dad had meant to me, and so she didn't judge me. A lot of people would think she was just as crazy as I was for going along with something like this, but no one knew me better than she did and she knew I wasn't a killer. I couldn't put my love for her into words, I could only hope my actions would continue to be enough.

She did make me promise not to tell a soul what I'd done, not even a confessional if I decided to switch from Baptist to Catholic. In the days following the shooting and wedding, the police department had issued several statements, as well as threats to the person or persons responsible. Seeing this, Melody had no illusions about what would happen if I ever got caught. Of course, the news and most social media outlets were screaming in outrage that there were no arrests or suspects in a white cop's murder.

Black on black crime or the shooting of an unarmed black man were common enough occurrences that the world didn't stop spinning for them. But the shit I'd done, even though some viewed it as Karma collecting her dues, was keeping the masses up at night. I didn't want to be callous, but it was comical. Almost every follower I had was hitting me on Facebook, Instagram and Twitter asking for my thoughts and feelings about Officer McDaniels' death. Wisely, I chose to keep my comments and innermost thoughts to myself.

ASAD

I tried to continue living as normally as I could just going to work and spending time with my wife. In the two weeks that had passed since we'd taken our vows I felt like we'd become closer, even though I'd always considered her my best friend. In the past I'd asked myself if I would ever get tired of being with the same woman, but everyday seemed brand new with Melody. I'd taken my mother's advice to heart, and that was why I was now waiting with a romantic dinner for two planned.

We had the house to ourselves because my mom had taken a mini vacation to her sister's house in Florida, needing a break from everything. I was kinda glad she was out of the house, because I could physically see the toll it was taking out on her to live with a ghost. No matter how many smiles you got from good memories they couldn't outnumber the tears shed because of the loss of that person.

"What's all this?" Melody asked, coming through the front door and stopping amongst the scattered rose petals beneath her feet.

"Just follow the path, baby," I called from my chair at the kitchen table.

I watched her sit her briefcase down and close the door before she stepped out of her three-inch heels and came toward me. The royal blue dress she had on was hugging her curves, causing me to lick my lips and contemplate whether or not dinner would be served on time.

"How is it you have been at work for eight hours, but you still look as fresh as the rose petals you're stepping on?" I asked.

"Aren't you sweet. I can't even be mad that you snuck out of work and left me hanging, but maybe you can explain why I'm walking on roses?"

"Oh, because *Coming to America* was on earlier and it gave me the idea," I replied laughing.

"Well, hopefully that's not wild goat you're cooking for me," she replied, finally coming to a stop in front of me and sitting on my lap.

"No goat. Just chicken," I told her in between kisses.

"I like chicken, but tell me what I did to deserve the royal treatment,"

"You woke up this morning, baby. That's enough for me."

"Aww…baby, that's so sweet. Now tell me what you did wrong," she replied laughing.

"I didn't do nothing. Wow, I can't believe how suspicious you are," I said feigning hurt.

"You're a man, baby, you've always done something, but I love you regardless."

"Well, thank you, sweetheart. Now hop up and sit in this chair across from me."

She did as I asked and I pulled my chair closer to hers so I could have her feet in my lap for me to massage.

"How was your day?" I asked.

"It doesn't matter, because I'm in absolute heaven now!"

"Of course it matters, baby. Besides, we've got time until dinner is done, so this is the conversation part of the night. Trust me, it won't be no talking later on, I promise you that," I warned, winking at her. My response made her smile, but I knew my woman and something was bothering her.

"Talk to me, baby," I coaxed.

"It's nothing, Stephon, just more dumb shit on Facebook, and a few people voiced their opinion at work today."

"What? Who?" I asked, feeling my blood begin to boil.

"Not employees, customers. I wanted to show my ass, but you know I would never do anything that could hurt the business."

"Fuck that! What was said?"

"Just slick comments about me being with you for the money," she replied vaguely.

My first instinct was still a protective one, but I couldn't hold in the laughter and that made her laugh.

"Who would say some dumb shit like that, and they must have no idea that you're rich," I replied.

"Just some nobody, baby. That's why it doesn't matter. Can we focus on our night together?"

"Yes, sweetheart, we can. Hold on while I check the food," I said releasing her feet, and heading to the kitchen to wash my hands.

Once I was sure her purple toenail polish wouldn't transfer off my hands into the food, I checked the cornbread. It was golden brown and the last thing to complete the feast of fried chicken, mashed potatoes and peas. I quickly made our plates and carried them back to the table.

"Mmm, is that your mom's cornbread?" Melody asked.

"You know I had to hit her up for the recipe. Go ahead and dig in while I grab our drinks," I said, picking out two wine glasses and taking the chilled red wine from the refrigerator.

"Ooh, and wine too?" she asked excitedly.

"Well if I get you tipsy enough maybe we can push the limits of freakiness in the bedroom tonight."

At first she stared blankly at me, and then she burst into laughter before taking a glass from my hand and holding it out for me to fill. The evening progressed with good food, laughter and a lot of flirting. Nothing between us ever seemed to get old, no matter how many times we did it. I loved that. Once the meal was complete I managed to talk Melody into a slow dance around the living room, knowing that I couldn't go wrong with a down-loaded mix of R. Kelly's greatest hits that I just happened to have on my phone.

"Mr. Harris, if I didn't know any better I'd think you were trying to seduce me."

"And you'd be absolutely right, Mrs. Harris, but it's not just for tonight. I plan to seduce you for the rest of our lives together," I said kissing her neck while my hands molded themselves to her juicy booty.

"Why don't you take me in the bedroom and finish your seduction?" she purred.

"Or we could start it here and see how many places we can do it all over the house," I suggested, squeezing her tighter.

Before she could respond our music was interrupted by my phone ringing. I'd already had my mind made up to ignore it, but then her phone started ringing in her briefcase by the door.

"That can't be a coincidence," I said, looking down into her eyes.

"Doubtful. The question is do we answer whoever it is or do we continue with our night?"

"You know what I wanna do," I replied smiling.

I could see the lust and the need in her eyes, but they didn't dampen the curiosity and I knew I wouldn't have her undivided attention until that animal was sated.

"Get your phone," I said laughing and releasing her from my grip.

Picking up my phone I saw that my missed call was from my mother, but I also had several notifications for messages from my Facebook page and Instagram. As soon as I opened the first message my heart dropped to my feet.

"Oh shit," Melody said coming back to me with her phone in her hand.

"I saw it too," I said.

"Another cop killing an unarmed black man. I mean damn when is this shit gonna stop?" she asked frustrated.

That was the million-dollar question. It seemed like no matter how blatant it was that these cops were committing murder, they were still getting away with the shit. The justice system was full of loopholes and favors that muh'fuckas owed one another, which ultimately kept real justice an illusion. I could say it was sad, but I was tired of being sad about a situation that didn't have to happen. I was angry. Based on the messages I was seeing there were a lot of people that were angry.

"This shooting was in Chattanooga, Tennessee and them niggas down there are barking like they ain't letting it slide," I said.

"Killing cops ain't the answer. It's fighting an uphill battle, because they have a license to kill, which basically puts them above the law."

"So then are we just supposed to roll over and die? We should just go back to being slaves then, because obviously our lives ain't our own," I replied seriously.

"That's not what I meant, babe. I'm simply saying that there has to be a better way than trying to kill every cop. All cops aren't bad, and you gonna remember that if there are no cops to enforce law and order who's gonna protect you," she reasoned.

"Like they're protecting me now," I replied sarcastically.

"Hold up, are we really fighting about this right now?" she asked.

I knew my war wasn't with her, but if she kept talking this nonviolent shit she'd make herself an easy target. I knew she sympathized with the situation because she loved my dad, but the reality was that this threat of violence would always be an abstract thing to her. She didn't have to live with the fear of being gunned down.

"Nah, we not fighting we're having an adult discussion, but I don't think you get it."

"How don't I get it, Stephon? You know what happened to your dad affected me too."

"I know it did, but you don't live in fear every time you get behind the wheel of a car. You're just like a lot of people that understand and comprehend, but you can't put these shoes on," I said, my voice rising slightly due to the high emotions running through me. Being in this skin I understood how hard being black was and that wasn't something I could translate to her through words. I knew she could feel my pain, but she probably would never understand it because she didn't have to live it.

"You're right, babe," she said coming to a stop in front of me. "But do you think killing cops is gonna somehow make me or others feel your pain?" she asked sincerely, her eyes conveying two parts love and one part compassion. I didn't know if she understood that this wasn't supposed to be about inflicting pain as much as getting justice, but maybe that was because I lost my own message along the way.

I had to admit she was right, but the reality of that truth sparked an idea that was too crazy to put into words. Could it really be that simple though? And if this was the way to shed some light on the situation and create more dialogue, did that mean it was the path I should take?

"I've known you for a long time, Stephon, and I know when you're in deep thought. Would you care to vocalize whatever has you literally licking your lips?" she asked.

I was still looking at it from different angles, but I already knew there was no way to bring the idea to her reasonably. Better to shoot from the hip.

"I've got an idea that will change everything, but I need you to trust me to work it out and then I'll bring it to you," I said. She was looking at me warily, but I didn't see mistrust in her eyes.

"I'll let you figure it out, because like you said I don't know the fear you live with," she replied. And neither did a lot of white people out there, but maybe it was time they did.

ASAD

CHAPTER EIGHT

We tried to rekindle the magic of the evening, but our focus was more occupied with suffering than sex. We lay in bed holding each other, neither of us speaking the swirling thoughts that occupied our minds in the moment. I felt like the plan of action I wanted to take was definitely a radical one, but it would open the eyes of the masses in a major way. How could I pass up an opportunity like that? I couldn't.

So now that I'd decided on my course of action, I needed a plan that wouldn't leave me dead or in prison forever. One step at a time, my mind turned over each piece of the thousand piece puzzle, unable to shut down even when I heard her breathing change as she found the lands of sleep. What I was getting ready to do would change or challenge every plan I'd ever made for my life, and that was a scary thing to contemplate.

There was no going back though. I think I'd always known that somewhere in the back of my mind, from the moment my dad was unjustly killed, change had been forced upon me, and this was what it looked like. Still, I wondered how the woman in my arms would feel about this change, this plan of action. I wasn't questioning her love or commitment to me, but this wasn't what she signed up for. So did I try to keep it a secret? Lies, even lies by omission, had a way of damaging even the strongest relationships and leaving them beyond repair.

I didn't want that for us. At the same time, I didn't want my mission to become her reason for mental instability. I weighed the pros and cons until I saw the black of night fade to purple and transform to bright orange, and I was still undecided about what to do. I guess love was funny like that, because it required brutal honesty, which wasn't always possible in the face of protection. In the end, I had to take it one step at a time until I had no choice but to tell her.

Watching the sunrise through my window signaled the first day of the rest of my life, and I intended to start it properly. I loved the way Melody felt in my arms and how she fit to me when we spooned with her back to my front. I loved the smell of strawberries in her hair and peaches on her skin, and how close we felt when we had sex in this position. I slid my leg slowly in between hers so as not to wake her too soon while positioning myself at the stairway to her heaven. Pushing inside her hard and fast just the way she liked, I heard her gasp as she squeezed my arm.

"Baby," she whispered in a momentary panic from being awakened this way.

"It's okay, I got you," I replied, holding her tighter while pulling out slowly only to dive back inside her with a pounding blow.

Using my hand that wasn't wrapped around her body, I lifted the hair from the back of her neck, kissing her there in a soft deliberate manner. When she arched her back and started moving with me I knew she was ready, and so I sunk my teeth into the spot I'd just kissed, loving how hard she came instantly.

"Again," she panted throwing it back at me.

I rolled her on her stomach, grabbing a fistful of her hair, and then pulled her up on all fours without coming out of her delicious treasures. For the next half hour, it was a battle of wills as I rode her hard, refusing to accept her surrender when she almost collapsed from the climax. I was a man possessed and determined, chasing the future until I finally lost all control.

"W…wh…what was that?" she asked, out of breath, but smiling as she laid down beside me.

"I just lo…love you, baby," I replied trying to catch my breath.

"I have no doubt that you love me, but damn you just tried to give me whiplash and put my head through a wall."

"That was me making up for last night," I said, playing with her nipples.

"Maybe we should have more conversations that end in a difference of opinion," she replied laughing.

"You couldn't handle it," I teased.

"Oh really? Well, I accept that challenge whenever you want to put it down like this again. In the meantime, I need to shower and get ready for work," she said, giving me a quick kiss and standing up.

She must've stood up too fast because she wobbled on unsteady legs before catching herself and running to the bathroom. Of course, I found that funny, and it made me want to poke out my chest with pride for giving it to her good.

"You okay, babe?" I called out.

Her reply was muffled by the sound of running water, but she had the right idea because it was time to make a move with my plans for the day. I may not have been a street nigga, but I had family all over the city that was 'bout that life. For the average muh'fucka it was too early to call or text, but I grabbed my phone off the nightstand and shot my cousin a message because I knew he was still on the block getting those early bird sales. David was my family on my dad's side, the oldest of my uncle Stephen's kids, which made him two years older than me.

We'd been close when we were young, but once my uncle overdosed on heroin five years ago David kinda drifted away to do his own thing. I still kept in touch just to make sure he was still living, or if I needed something only the streets could provide. Today was a day for the latter so I hit him up and told him I'd meet him at the Waffle House on Southwest. I didn't know how much I planned to tell him about what I had in mind even though I was sure nothing would surprise him. I just didn't wanna make him a co-defendant. He texted me back A.S.A.P and told me he'd be there by nine a.m., which meant I had about an hour and a half to get myself together.

Getting out of bed, I went to my closet and grabbed a black Hustle Gang t-shirt with a matching hoodie, a pair of denim polo jeans, and my butter Timbs. Laying all that on the bed, I grabbed a pair of boxers from my dresser drawer and went to join my wife in the shower. She was probably gonna be pissed that I was taking the day off, so I was trying to get my excuse ready, but what I heard outside the bathroom door pushed all that from my mind. Ordinarily, I had a weak stomach and I couldn't be around someone throwing up, but knowing that was my wife on the other side of that door made me throw caution to the wind.

"Baby, you okay?" I asked opening the door without knocking.

The sight that met me would've had me turned on at any other time because I had an eye popping view of Melody's ass and more, but her heaving was not sexy.

"I'm fine," she whined, trying to catch her breath.

Some women threw up, and other women cried when they threw up. On the rare occasions when I found myself in this exact position I felt so bad because Melody was a crier. I hated to see her cry.

"Are you sick? Do I need to take you to the hospital? Was it the wine last night?" I asked in a rapid-fire manner.

Her immediate response was to blow more chunks into the toilet, forcing me to turn away before I added to the growing mess. I could already feel the tingling in my throat, which was a clear signal that I needed to remove myself from this situation, but I knew I couldn't. In sickness and in health was part of the vows we'd taken.

"I-I'm okay," she said wiping her mouth and flushing the toilet.

I let her hair go as she made her way to the sink and immediately began to brush her teeth.

"You're obviously sick, so you're gonna take the day off and go to the doctors..."

"I don't need to go to the doctor, babe. Sex was a little rough this morning, that's all," she replied, trying to smile in an effort to ease my concern.

"Since when does rough sex make you puke?"

"My guess is I would've puked anyway, but the way you tried to give us shaken baby syndrome didn't help."

"Oh whatever, it's probably something you ate last night or...wait a minute, shaken baby syndrome? You said give *us* shaken baby syndrome, so does that mean yo...you're..." I hesitated to say the word partly in fear of what it meant and everything that came with it. I didn't need to say it though; I was looking in her eyes through the mirror and the truth was as plain as the smile on her face.

"W-we're gonna have a baby?" I whispered, willing my legs to hold me up as I moved to stand right behind her.

"Yeah, I think so. Are you okay with that?" she asked searching my eyes for the truth and security my words couldn't convey.

"I'm more than okay with that," I said turning her around to face me. "I love you, Melody, and our child was created in love."

"Yeah, it was. It looks like I'll be taking online college courses this semester," she said, rubbing her stomach and laughing.

I put my hand over hers, imagining the day when I'd feel my little boy or girl kicking and communicating from within. I could feel the tears working their way down my cheeks, but they were in good company of the smile I was wearing from ear-to-ear. I was gonna be a daddy. That thought reinforced in me the conclusions I'd come to in the early morning hours. There was no way I could bring my child into a world that condemned them based on skin color alone without at least doing my part to affect change. Every decision my father made was to make life better for me and my mother, and now it was my turn to do the same thing.

"If you wanna take classes online I'll do it with you, but can you please spit and rinse so I can kiss you already!" I said, growing more excited by the minute.

She did as I asked and then opened her mouth to me for an all-out assault. I guided her into the shower and this time I was extremely gentle with loving her body. Afterwards we bathed each other and I convinced her to schedule an OB/GYN appointment for today. According to her, she knew she was pregnant because she missed her period and got sick a few times, but I wanted her to have an official check-up. Once we got out of the shower she made the call and got an eleven a.m. spot with the doctor. I agreed to meet her there so we could find out everything together.

"I want you to drive my mom's truck instead of your car," I said, putting my clothes on.

"Why?"

"Because an Escalade is a lot safer than a Ferrari Spyder if you get in an accident. Your sole focus in life is keeping my baby safe," I informed her.

"Oh Lord, I see now how you're gonna act this entire pregnancy," she said, rolling her eyes as she went to the closet to find something to wear.

"Not just this pregnancy either," I replied, pulling on my boots and checking to make sure I had everything I needed.

"Whatever, I'll take the truck. Are you taking my car then?"

"Nah, I'm going to visit my cousin and I can't roll through the hood like that. I'ma take my dad's car," I said.

This revelation brought her out of the closet wearing only her panties, bra and a worried expression on her face.

"You…you're gonna drive your dad's car?" she asked hesitantly.

No one had been behind the wheel of the car since I'd had it cleaned months ago. We just kept it in the garage. I couldn't say I was over what happened in that car, but I was done being afraid.

"Yes, baby, I'm gonna drive my dad's car. It's okay and I'm working through it, but trust me you'll be the first to know if shit gets too difficult," I said sincerely.

"Okay. Be safe and I'll meet you at the doctor's office later on," she said, coming to give me a kiss before I left.

"I love you, baby," I said.

"I love you, too."

Part of me didn't wanna leave her side even for a moment. I wanted to spend the day waiting on her hand and foot, showering her with love and showing her how grateful I was to have her and our child. I couldn't do that though because I had to do my part in hopes that my son or daughter might know the true meaning of equality. Grabbing the keys to the Mercedes from the bowl on the kitchen counter I made my way into the garage. I took a deep breath, got behind the wheel, and started the car. For a moment, I simply sat there wondering if I could do this.

I felt like if I wasn't supposed to do it I would've got some type of sign from my dad in this moment. After five minutes of hearing nothing more than the engine purr I hit the garage door clicker on the visor to open the door and I backed out. It felt weird to be behind the wheel, because my dad never let me drive this baby. But I would get used to it since my mom said it was my car now. No one knew about my Crown Vic, and I still hadn't bothered to get my wrecked '95 Impala fixed, but it didn't seem as important as it once had.

I made it to the Waffle House in thirty minutes, which put me about ten minutes early. But I spotted my cousin's smoke gray Navigator in the parking lot, which meant he was inside. For a muh'fucka doing illegal transactions, he didn't try very hard to keep a low profile. His truck was sitting on twenty-eight inch rims and the tint on all the windows only did so much to block out the glow of his T.V. screens. The best part of his truck had to be the system though. You definitely heard him before you saw him. I backed my car into the space next to his, locked it up, and headed inside. I wasn't surprised to see him in the company of some bubble gum poppin,' booty short wearin,' hood booger, but this one was kinda cute in the face.

"What's up, cuzzo?" I asked giving him dap.

"Ain't shit my nig. Feeding my face before I get back to the trap music."

"From the looks of shit business is good," I said.

I admired the platinum and diamond teeth taking up space in the bottom of his mouth. The Jesus piece he wore around his neck matched it perfectly. Most people thought we were brothers because we were the same height, weight and complexion. He had hazel eyes instead of my plain browns though, and he rocked a high-top fade in comparison to my low cut.

"Yeah, it's good. Why you looking for a career change?" he asked laughing.

"Nah, bruh, you know that ain't me. I got some shit I need to holla at you about," I said taking a seat in the booth.

"Talk to me, cuz," he said, going back to the plate of chicken and waffles in front of him.

"I need a couple favors," I began, leaning across the table to minimize the ability to eavesdrop.

"I need another pistol, a Glock .40 this time. I also need somebody to do some work on the Crown Vic."

"The gun ain't a problem, but what type of work you talkin' 'bout getting done on your car?" he asked.

"Big daddy, I need..."

"Bitch! Didn't I tell you to wait in the truck?" David asked, clearly frustrated about being disobeyed and interrupted.

She turned on her heels and didn't say another word on her way out to the parking lot.

"I hate hardheaded females. Finish what you was saying, cuz. What do you need done to your ride?"

"I need a bright light added to the side, lights in the grill, Virginia tags that won't come back stolen..."

"Hold up, my nigga. It sounds to me like you're trying to turn your Crown Vic into an undercover cop car. Why the fuck would you wanna do that? You might get shot in the hood rolling around in some shit like that," he warned.

"Trust me, you don't wanna know what I'm on."

"A Glock .40 and a fake cop car. It sounds like your crazy ass is about to impersonate the law, fam, but I know that's not it, right?" he asked, pushing his plate away and giving me his undivided attention.

David was family, but this was too big to trust with anyone. A hustler's days were numbered, so who was to say he didn't get jammed up and need a way out? I couldn't let that be me, especially with a baby on the way.

"I know what I'm doing, bruh," I said.

"And what's that?"

"They gotta learn, David, but they won't until they feel our pain."

ASAD

CHAPTER NINE

One Week Later

Melody wore the glow of pregnancy well. She tried to tell me it was my imagination because she was only eight weeks pregnant so she wasn't glowing, but I knew radiant when I saw it. Even laying in bed with her now, the room awash in moonlight, her skin shone with a fluorescence that wasn't there before. She was absolutely beautiful, and according to our doctor's visit she was as healthy as can be. Much to her annoyance the morning sickness would become more frequent and last well into the second trimester, but the doctor assured her that she was still healthy.

So far we'd kept the news to ourselves, wanting to make sure we were out of the immediate danger zone of a miscarriage before we got everyone all worked up. There was no doubt that our baby would be loved and embraced by both sides of the family, and we were definitely planning to spoil our little one. It was still hard to wrap my mind around the fact that I was gonna be a dad. I could remember when I was younger how there were so many speeches given at school about babies having babies, and how that negativity impacted one's future.

And now the teen pregnancy rate was down, but cops killing kids was quickly becoming a rising thing. They didn't want us to row up if we came from the mud. I knew Melody and I would be considered statistics for becoming teenage parents, but I'd rather contribute to the giving of a new life and hopefully give my child a chance at equality. For me that journey would start tonight. It hadn't taken more than a few days for my cousin to have the changes made to my Crown Vic, and he delivered on the guns with a bonus in the form of a bulletproof vest belonging to the Virginia State Troopers.

With the physical preparations taken care of I'd focused on the mental preparation, and tonight was the night shit became real instead of hypothetical. I'd thought I was gonna have to slip Melody a sleeping pill or something, but I was concerned that it would hurt my baby. In the end I'd elected to tire her out the old fashioned way by having her work on our latest interior design job for a house in Georgetown, and then making love to her several times after dinner. When it was all said and done she was lying next to me snoring lightly, and all I could do was hope she slept through the night.

When the clock struck two a.m. I eased out of bed and went down the hallway to the laundry room where I got dressed. Normal State Troopers wore a blue and gray combination uniform, but since I was moving around under the cover of night I'd chosen a pair of plain black cargo pants, a black long sleeve knit shirt, and some black combat boots. I had a shoulder holster for the Glock .40 and David had given me a Chrome .357 Smith and Wesson Revolver for the holster on my hip.

I wouldn't strap my guns and vest on until I got to the car though. Once I was dressed and had what I needed I disabled the alarm and was out the back door, becoming one with the night. With my car looking like an official police car now I'd decided that keeping it on the street wasn't a good idea, but luckily for me an old man rented me his garage without questions. When I stepped into the alley behind my house I kept going straight, crossing through one of my neighbor's back yard and going one block left to the garage.

It was old and dilapidated, but it would serve its purpose. After looking around to make sure I wasn't being watched I pulled the car cover off and tossed it in the corner. There sat a black on black '98 Ford Crown Victoria sedan with tinted windows and a police spotlight. I went to the trunk and put on both gun holsters with the matching hardware, and strapped on my bulletproof vest.

I'd chosen a black wool hat and some open fingered black leather gloves as appropriate props to complete my outfit, and once I had everything on I got on the move.

I'd already chosen to operate outside of D.C. because I wasn't trying to shit where I slept, plus I knew handling business in Virginia was more poetic and fitting. With this being my first outing I didn't wanna go too far or stay gone too long, so I pointed my ride towards I-395 until I could switch over to Route 66. The worst thing that could happen was for me to come in contact with any other cops, so I kept my eyes open and my speed at the limit.

Regular police cars had radar detectors in them, so I'd added one to mine, but I didn't wanna risk alerting anybody of my presence. The traffic was light and all I'd seen so far were single white woman or cars full of black people. It crossed my mind to pull over somewhere and wait, and after thirty minutes of driving I was just getting ready to give into the notion when I spotted them. Two white boys in a dark blue Yukon Denali merged onto the highway about five cars ahead of me. I felt my adrenaline pumping as I hit the lights and the sirens, and got right behind them until they pulled off to the side of the road. I checked the Glock to make sure it was fully loaded with one in the chamber before I stepped out of the car. I kept my arm pressed to my right leg with the gun out of sight, constantly scanning both sides of the highway, knowing I only had minutes to do this right.

"Was I speeding, Officer?" the driver asked when I got to his window.

"Nope. Wrong place, wrong time," I said, raising the gun into view and squeezing off three rounds quickly.

I hit the driver in the temple and the passenger in the forehead and throat. To run would definitely raise suspicions because cops didn't run unless they were chasing someone, so I walked as casually as I could back to my car. Once I was behind the wheel I turned off the lights and sirens and merged with traffic, taking the fifth exit I came to in order to turn around. It was hard for me to wait that long, but just in case cameras were checking I didn't want my car to show up so quick as to be suspicious. I had no doubt that when news of the double murder broke there would be people who remembered themselves being on this stretch of highway at this particular time.

Some of them might even remember the flashing lights off a cop car pulling the deceased over. The American public would do the math that was laid before them and that would equate to a traffic stop that resulted in two more homicides. Only this time the victims were white. My goal was simply to change the narrative of the story black people were living, or maybe I just wanted to change the narrator. Maybe if white people knew fear when they got behind the wheel of their cars they'd open their eyes and see the bigger picture.

As I came up on the scene of what I'd just done I saw the truck still sitting in the same spot with its lights on, and probably its engine still running. If I was lucky no cop would happen upon them until after sunrise, but either way I felt safe because I was heading back into D.C. An hour after I'd murdered two men in cold blood I was standing under the heat of cascading water in the cocoon of my bathroom. I felt so alive that I thought my entire body was humming with unseen electricity, and it made me wonder if this was how people felt when they did drugs.

By the time I finished my shower the sun was coming up so I put on a pair of boxers and went to the kitchen to make my wife breakfast in bed. I kept the menu simple with eggs, bacon, toast and orange juice because I didn't want her morning sickness to hit her before she could digest her meal. Once her plate was made I put it, her utensils, and her glass of juice on a tray and carried it into the bedroom. She was still sleeping peacefully and I hated to wake her up, but it had to be done.

"Baaaby," I said softly. She stirred, but didn't open her eyes.

"Mrs. Harris," I said sitting next to her on the bed.

"Hmm."

"Wake up, sweetheart."

"Is that bacon I smell?" she asked with her eyes still closed.

"It is."

"Did you cook me breakfast?" she asked popping one eye open.

"I did, now sit up and eat before it gets cold," I told her.

After stretching in a way that had me thinking about dessert instead of breakfast, she propped herself up in bed and took the tray I offered.

"Aww, you're gonna spoil me," she said giving me a quick kiss before she dug in.

"That's my job, babe."

"And you're damn good at it," she replied around a mouthful of eggs.

"Does that mean you're gonna share some with me?" I asked. Her response was to laugh while she shook her head no before attacking a strip of bacon.

"You know I love you, baby, and I've definitely got something you can eat, but my bacon ain't it," she said.

"Very funny," I replied reaching for a piece of bacon only to have my hand slapped away.

"You're serious?" I asked.

"As a nympho in a room full of dicks."

I had to laugh, but I left her to her food while I went to the closet to get dressed for work. In the back of my mind I was wondering if the cops had discovered what I'd left on the side of the road, but I knew I had to proceed like this was a normal day.

"Babe, I'm getting in the shower. Can you pick me out something to wear?" she called out.

Not a lot of women would trust their man's opinion with matters of fashion, but Melody only dressed to impress me. I laid out one of her form fitting red dresses to match the tie that was going with my gray suit and white shirt. This way we were prepared for the meetings of the day and still sophisticated enough for an afternoon power lunch. By the time she got out of the shower I was dressed to impress with matching Gators on my feet, and a plan of action in my mind for my next move.

Seeing her naked and dripping wet almost had us late for work, but she put me off with a promise of a wild night later. While she got dressed I made myself a quick bacon and egg sandwich and checked a few media news sights to find out what the morning scoop was. I didn't find what I was looking for as I felt a surge of impatience, but I managed to fight it down.

"You ready to go, babe?" she asked coming into the kitchen.

"Yeah, but you're driving."

We decided to take my mom's Escalade, discussing whether or not it was too soon to buy some type of family vehicle. She was open to getting some type of truck, but I was thinking minivans. If I had it my way, she'd be barefoot and pregnant for at least the next five years. Of course, she laughed her ass off at that idea and told me to step into 2016. We made it to work at seven forty-five a.m., which left us fifteen minutes before our first meeting with a couple interested in having us do the interior design for their new townhouse in Northern Virginia.

In the front of the store is where all the paint samples were and people could browse, but in the back were our offices where people scheduled to meet us and discuss specific projects. My dad had built the company from a simple store that sold paint and offered to apply it when necessary to a business that was frequently mentioned in different home improvement and design magazines. Now it was up to me and Melody to take it into the future and build something for our kids to inherit.

"I'ma grab some coffee and meet you in your office," Melody said.

"Bring me some coffee and you'll have tea, thank you very much," I replied, going in the opposite direction of her.

"Good morning, Mr. Harris, the Jenson family is waiting for you in your office," my secretary said.

"Okay, Mrs. Jacobs."

Diane Jacobs had been my father's secretary for ten years, and it had been a blessing for her to agree to continue working with us after his death. She was a black grandmotherly type with white hair and a kind smile, but that only hid her quick tongue until you pissed her off. Once she was mad you had a four foot eight inch, one hundred and thirty pound ball of fire on your hands. Shit, the only reason she was calling me Mr. Harris is because there were customers in the immediate vicinity.

"Mr. and Mrs. Jenson, I'm sorry you had to wait," I said coming into my office.

They were seated in the cushy leather chairs directly in front of my cherry wood desk. My office wasn't very big, but it was tastefully decorated with wall-to-wall burgundy carpeting that matched both the chairs in front of my desk and the leather swivel I claimed as my own. The rest of the features were done in gold, mainly because my father had been a diehard Washington Redskin fan. I kept the pictures of him with various players at different functions up on the wall along with the family portrait with my mom and I. Leaving everything the same made me feel closer to my dad.

"It's no problem, Mr. Harris, we're early," Mr. Jensen said, rising to shake my hand. I shook it firmly and air kissed his wife's when she offered it up.

"Can I offer either of you something to drink?" I asked.

"We're fine, thank you. Your secretary made sure we were comfortable while we waited. We wouldn't have been so early except the detour got us into the city sooner than expected," Mrs. Jensen said.

"Detour?"

"Oh yeah, out on 66 just past Arlington," Mr. Jensen chimed in.

"Sorry you were kept waiting," Melody said, coming into the office and shaking hands with our clients after sitting our cups on my desk.

"Oh, it was no problem, we were early and we were just telling your husband about the road blocks," Mr. Jensen replied.

"Road blocks?" Melody asked.

"Yeah, there's a detour on Route 66 because the police have a section of the highway blocked off on both sides," Mrs. Jensen continued.

"Why, was there some type of accident?" Melody asked.

"No child, not an accident at all. The story on the radio was that there's been another killing during a traffic stop. But this time the men killed were white."

CHAPTER TEN

Two Weeks Later

"...Thanks, Marv. This is Jessica Carlton with Channel Three News coming to you live from the scene of the latest traffic stop gone horribly wrong. I'm here in Richmond, Virginia on Highway 81, where the Virginia State Police found a grey 2012 Mercedes S500 parked this morning at three a.m. Inside they discovered another gruesome double homicide. At this time the victim's names have not been released because their families haven't been notified, but we do know that it was a man and a woman this time, approximately thirty years of age. With these latest two victims that raises the body count to eight in a span of three weeks, and with no suspects or solid leads people in Richmond, Arlington, and Manassas, Virginia are starting to voice their fears about driving.

"A lot of people still remember the D.C. sniper attacks over a decade ago, and they're comparing the fear they felt then with what's taking place now. There seems to be no rhyme or reason to these attacks, and no connection other than the description of an undercover cop car either dark blue or black being in the area. Could this really be the workings of a rogue cop who took an oath to protect and serve us from senseless violence? The president is demanding answers, while leaders like Jesse Jackson and Rev. Al Sharpton ask the question of why everyone is so angry now opposed to when it's innocent black people dying. There are a lot of questions, but not a lot of answers, and no one it seems is safe. I'm Jessica Carlton, Channel Three News, Richmond, Virginia..."

"Ladies, I'm home!" I called out coming through the door.

"We're in here, honey," my mom yelled.

Closing the door and taking my jacket off, I headed towards the sound of her voice and the T.V. I walked in the living room to find my wife and mother both sitting on the couch with their feet on the coffee table, a bowl of barbeque potato chips between them.

"Don't you two look comfortable," I said kissing first my wife on the cheek and then my mom.

"We are comfortable, thank you very much. How'd the estimate go?" Melody asked.

I had to take a quick two-day trip to Stanton, Virginia to see a client's home and give them an estimate for how much it would cost to redo everything. I'd also made a little detour down into the capital of Virginia and left a gift for them, but I wouldn't bore my wife and mother with those details.

"Everything went smoothly. It was weird at first because I've never had to do one of those without Dad, but it made me feel grown up," I replied.

"You are grown up, sweetheart. Ever since your father passed you've stepped up and been absolutely amazing. I hope you know he would be proud of you," my mom said, trying not to get choked up on all the emotions she was obviously feeling.

"Thanks, Mom," I said kissing her on top of her head.

"So, what have you two been doing?" I asked, hoping to lighten up the mood a little.

"Exactly what you see here, feeding our faces with comfortable sweatpants and t-shirts on," Melody replied laughing.

"And what have you been eating wife?"

"Whatever she craves and if you're smart you'll keep your mouth shut about it," my mom said.

We hadn't waited as long as we'd planned to reveal the news about the pregnancy, mainly because my mother was neither blind nor stupid. Our families had been thrilled though. Melody's dad had actually got teary eyed. The fact that there was a life growing inside her still filled me with so much joy every time I thought about it. In six months, I would meet my baby, my legacy, and I couldn't wait!

"I'm smarter than I look, Mom. Besides a wise woman once told me that a happy wife equaled a happy life."

"I second that notion, baby, in fact you should make that your motto for life," Melody said smiling.

"Whatever you say, my queen," I replied, taking a bow, which made both women laugh.

"Well, I was thinking about taking you out for dinner, but..."

"It's almost eight p.m. so you should just order in. Plus, I don't want you two out driving at night," my mom insisted.

"What? Why?" I asked.

"Well, just before you came in we were watching the news and there's been another killing on the highway down in Richmond, Virginia," she replied.

"Mom that's in Virginia, and it's white people being killed so..."

"Well, in case you haven't noticed, your pregnant wife is white. We don't know what this wacko is thinking, but it's entirely possible that he or she would have a problem with an interracial couple, given all the tension between blacks and whites."

"Why do you automatically assume that whoever is doing this is a wacko? Maybe he or she is just speaking for everyone who's tired of unarmed black men and kids being killed without consequence," I said calmly.

"That's not how you speak out against injustice," Melody said.

"Really? How then, because I'm still waiting for justice for my father."

Melody opened her mouth to speak, but thought better of it and said nothing. For a moment, my mom stared off into space and I suddenly realized how insensitive my comments were.

"Mom, I'm sorry. I..."

"It's ok, Stephon, I get it. There's not a day that passes when I don't miss your father. There's not a day when I don't ask god why, or will this pain ever go away, but it's not a pain I wish on others. That's not what my husband would want either."

"No, he may not, but he also wouldn't want his son to die as he did. Nobody cares when black men die. Shit they barely care how we lived, which is why black history month is one month out of twelve. I mean think about it, Mom, it goes all the way back to the establishment of this great country. Christopher Columbus steals a whole goddamn country from the Indians, but labels it as discovery and he gets a holiday. But if my black ass steals a candy bar because I'm hungry I'm labeled a menace to society and thrown in jail. There is no justice for a black man, because there is no value of life, but all of a sudden white people are dying and the world is paying attention," I said.

"So you believe the end justifies the means?" Melody asked.

"If it leads to real and productive conversation about equality and justice for all, then yes," I replied.

"But how would you feel if that was your wife that was shot in the face in Manassas?"

"The same way I felt when it was my father's," I said quietly.

Again, my mom got this far off look on her face, but my wife was looking at me directly in the eyes. Her stare wasn't accusatory, more so inquisitive like she might have been seeing me for the first time. I realized that if we continued with this topic of conversation I might tip my hand or at the very least say something completely insensitive.

"Listen, enough talk of death and justice. I understand you're worried, Mom, so we won't go out, but I offer a compromise. How about I go get us something from the carry-out?" I offered.

"Ooh, I want a foot-long steak and cheese with extra onions, fries and a slice of apple pie," Melody said, rubbing her stomach.

"Anything else?' I asked laughing, amused at the sudden increase in her appetite due to the pregnancy.

"A chocolate shake would be nice. What about you, Mom?" she asked.

"I want some beef and broccoli with extra egg rolls and duck sauce."

"Coming right up. You ladies just sit back and relax and try to find us a good movie to watch on Netflix," I said, kissing them both on the top of the head before retreating the way I came.

During the entire ride to get the food I couldn't help wondering if either my mother or wife could truly see the bigger picture. True enough our last president had been black and that was a historical thing for African Americans, but there was still a long way to go before we saw the fair treatment we were entitled to. For obvious reasons I'd kept a close eye on the news coverage and reactions the killings had generated, and it had been just what I expected. There was fear, and outrage and demands that the killer be brought to justice. There were FBI agents, investigating cops, and politicians using words like Marshall Law for the entire state of Virginia until the killer was caught.

And on the flip side you still had people protesting and speaking out for groups like Black Lives Matter asking why all the attention and concern was given to white victims and not all victims. Maybe I should have felt some remorse for the things I had done, but in this moment I felt hope because now the needed conversation could not be had behind closed doors or where our voice couldn't be heard, it was starting to feel like a revolution and that brought a certain excitement. I'd noticed in the passing months how a lot of people liked to bring up the slogan 'All Lives Matter' whenever someone mentioned 'Black Lives Matter,' but those same people didn't like that statement thrown in their faces.

On my way back from the carry-out, I listened to a news report that was talking about how more people were applying for and getting permits so they could travel armed. My first thought was that if it was black folks doing it then we were only giving the police another excuse to shoot us on sight. Not that they needed a reason.

"I'm back," I said coming through the door with the bags of food.

"We're right where you left us," Melody called out.

"You could've at least got the plates," I said, shaking my head as I sat the food on the coffee table.

"Plates? For what?" my mom asked, pulling her container of food out of the bag and passing Melody her sub.

"Baby, can you bring me a glass of ginger ale?" Melody asked.

"And bring me some tea," my mom chimed in.

It was on the tip of my tongue to make a smartass comment about being their servant, but I saw no scenario in which that would help me. My best bet was to smile and nod, which I did on my way to get their drinks.

"Will there be anything else, madams?" I asked once I'd returned and passed them their drinks.

"No, my darling husband, but I want you to sit right here next to me so we can watch this movie," Melody insisted, sliding to the middle of the couch and sitting my own foot-long steak and cheese in front of me.

"What we watching?" I asked, getting comfortable and unwrapping my food.

"*The Birth of a Nation*," my mom replied.

"And who picked that movie?" I asked looking at Melody.

"Your wife did," my mom replied.

There was a light in Melody's eyes that looked challenging, but I wasn't quite sure what it meant, so I let it go. Once we were settled and everyone was eating my mom started the movie. From the beginning, I was hooked just from a historical standpoint because schools always gave a sanitized version of slavery and how it affected black people, especially on these shores. It took creative minds not afraid to shine a light in the darkness to really put the truth on the big screen where the world couldn't keep hiding from it. So many people liked to believe that slavery and the days of being a second-class citizen were so far behind us, but those days were still happening and would keep happening if we didn't do something to affect change.

There was a scene in the movie when the character playing Nat Turner was leading a slave revolt and he screamed the word rebel as he led the charge against his oppressors. I felt my skin come alive with goose bumps and I had to fight to stay seated. I mean the struggle was real, and in that moment I had a new found respect for every slave that lost their life for refusing to kneel.

"Wow, that was a helluva movie," my mom said once the credits were rolling.

"Powerful," Melody commented.

I simply shook my head, still seeing the movie where there were now names scrolling up the T.V. screen.

"Well, I thank you, children, for a lovely evening, but I'm taking my tired, old butt to bed."

"Night, Mom," Melody and I said in unison.

"Baby, you want me to put your half of sub in the refrigerator?" I asked.

"Nope, bring it in the bedroom with us," she replied gathering the trash together.

I knew not to comment or argue because her cravings were real, and this would save me a trip in the middle of the night. After making sure the house was locked up and the alarm was on, I made my way to the bedroom where I found her lying in bed naked.

"You waiting on me?" I asked, sitting her sandwich on her nightstand and getting undressed.

"Of course, but not for what you're thinking."

"Oh really, well what's on your mind?" I asked getting under the covers and pulling her close to me.

"A lot of stuff. I'm wondering if we're doing the right thing by bringing a child into the world in this day and age," she said.

"What do you mean?"

"I mean there's so much hate, so much killing. How far have we really come from the timeframe that movie was based on? And we're bringing a mixed child into the world and that means he or she has the potential to have it harder than most because of the racial divide in society."

"I understand what you're saying, sweetheart, but I feel like our child's success will depend on how well we prepare them for the world that awaits. As long as we're conscious we have the ability to make sure our child's conscious," I replied.

"Would you tell our child that there's nothing wrong with the killings going on right now?" she asked, looking up at me.

"Which killings?"

"Don't be an ass, you know exactly what I'm talking about," she said.

I could feel my heart beating in my ears and I had to tell myself to calm the fuck down before she felt my heart racing too.

"I'm always gonna explain right from wrong to our child, babe, but what's going on right now has many layers to it, so I think that conversation would only happen when the maturity level warranted it," I replied calmly. She kept looking at me for a second before she responded.

"What the fuck are you talking about now? Killing is wrong period, and our child should know that from day one. Whoever is out there killing people is wrong no matter what the motivation is, I mean for God's sake, eight innocent people are dead!" she said, clearly frustrated.

I could see there was no winning this argument, and this damn sure wasn't the time to confess my sins to her. She just didn't get it.

"You're right, sweetheart, and I know we'll teach our child right and wrong. It's our responsibility to make sure he or she doesn't simply survive, but thrives in this world and becomes better than us," I said.

"Exactly. But I'm still worried about..."

I silenced her worries with a kiss as I pulled her on top of me in one smooth motion. Every time she opened her mouth to speak I initiated a dance between her tongue and mine, until she finally realized talking was no longer on the menu of tonight's activities. Within seconds I was inside her, lost in her strength and passion as she rode me into the night at a slow gallop.

We both had to work to contain our excitement in ways that we hadn't when we had the house to ourselves. Still there was an explosion of magnitude and fireworks that left us both breathless and weak. As usual, it didn't take fifteen minutes before her deep breathing became light snoring, but I was too wound up to sleep. I wanted to go out, but I knew I didn't need to go out. I'd done what needed to be done and now there was more than one conversation going on.

Wasn't that the goal? So wasn't that enough? Even as I said yes I was slipping from the bed and tiptoeing to my closet to get dressed. Within ten minutes I was behind the wheel of my Crown Vic trying to decide where I was going, and what to do when I got there. I got on I-495 and just cruised, liking the way I was able to blend in because there was still some traffic out due to the fact that it was only one a.m.

Before I knew it, I was coming up on the Springfield, Virginia exit, and as fate would have it there was a van driven by a white guy with a church's logo on the side that merged onto the highway in front of me. I couldn't see inside the van, but given the time of night the odds were slim that any passengers were on board. After two miles of following I hit my lights and sirens to pull over. Of course, the driver did just that, but I had to take a minute before I got out because traffic was suddenly heavy which meant an increased change for potential witnesses.

Finally, I stepped out the car, as always my pistol was to my side as I headed in the direction of the driver side door. I hadn't taken more than three steps when the flashing lights took on a new sequence. I knew what this meant, but I still took my time turning around so I could now conceal my pistol from a different view. There was now a car behind my car and as the door swung open I saw an all too familiar logo that read State Trooper. The real cops were here, and that made shit interesting.

CHAPTER ELEVEN

I had a number of decisions to make, and I had only seconds to make them. The odds were good that his dashboard cam had already got my car license plates, make and model, not to mention a shot of me from a distance. Hopefully, the image was too distorted given the light show that was happening between our cars. So the first decision I had to make was who would be my victim tonight, because I didn't see any scenario where I killed everybody and got away. The driver of the van couldn't see more than silhouettes behind him, which made identifying me almost impossible. It was obvious that the cop was the immediate threat, but the element of surprise was mine if I chose to seize it. I had no other choice.

"I could use a hand," I said, hoping to disarm him with the thought of camaraderie.

He stepped out of his cruiser with one hand on the butt of his service revolver and a flashlight in the other hand. He was trying to approach in a nonchalant manner, but I still saw his sweep of the flashlight across the back of my car as he neared the front of his. Ultimately, his suspicions made my decision easier. Before he could get any closer I raised my pistol and double tapped two shots into his head, rushing towards him even as his body slumped and rolled off the hood of his car.

I heard the van accelerate into traffic behind me, which was a good thing. Quickly, I checked for a pulse and then ran back to my car so I could pop the trunk. I hadn't planned for this exact situation, but after my first outing I'd realized the danger in going to the gas station and risking putting my car on camera for later identification. Based on that, I'd made the decision to keep at least three full gas cans with me in my trunk, and it was now that I removed one of those in hopes of saving my life.

I sat the gas can down before I heaved the cop's body into my trunk and slammed it closed. With every second that passed I could feel myself wanting to freak out more, but I took one deep breath after another and focused on what I had to do. I took the gas can and went to the passenger side of the dead cop's car, needing to put something between me and the passing traffic. Opening the passenger door, I noticed the push lighter in the console and I smashed it under my palm before I began soaking the inside of the cruiser with gas.

It seemed like the longest thirty seconds in the world before that lighter sprang back out, but as soon as it did I wedged it in between the passenger seat cushions and I was gone. I tossed the empty gas can on the passenger side floor of my car as I jumped behind the wheel, killed the lights and sirens, and sped off. When I was about a hundred feet away I could see the orange, flames mixing with the still flashing blue lights, but I knew I wasn't out of danger.

I had no idea what to do with the body in my trunk, but the one thing I did know was that I wasn't gonna try to figure it out in Virginia. I had to get back to D.C. A.S.A.P! I got off at the first exit and wasted no time getting back on the highway headed in the opposite direction, but to my dismay there was already another cop car on the scene of the one I'd left engulfed in flames. Common sense said maintain the same speed as the flow of traffic to avoid drawing attention to myself, but common sense went out the window and my foot had the peddle to the floor. Grabbing my phone, I dialed a number of the only person I knew could help me out in this situation.

"Yo?" he answered on the fourth ring.

"It's Stephon, where you at?"

"I'm working, cuzzo. What you doing calling this late?"

"David, I'm in trouble and I need your help," I said quickly.

"Where you at?" he asked.

"Just tell me where to meet you."

"I'm in Southeast of Minnesota Avenue, but I'll meet you at the corner of 39th," he replied.

"I'll be there in twenty minutes," I said, hanging up. I turned on my radar detector, because I had no intentions of letting off the gas in the slightest. My mind raced with regrets for not trusting my instincts about not coming out tonight. I was getting sloppy and reckless for no damn reason! Hindsight may have been twenty-twenty, but the one thing I knew with absolute certainty going forward was that I was gonna lay low for a while. Maybe even take a vacation with the wife before the baby was born.

First things first, I had to get myself out of this messy ass situation. I made it to the rendezvous point in nineteen minutes flat, pulling up right behind David's truck. Careful to keep my eyes open to my surroundings, I removed my bulletproof vest and both holsters before stepping out of the car and climbing into his passenger seat.

"Why the fuck do you smell like gas, my nigga, and why would you meet me driving that car?" he asked, clearly irritated.

"It's a long story. Right now I need your help in a major way," I said.

"Spit it out, nigga, I'm already missing sales because I'm sitting here with your ass."

"I need your help to get rid of a-a body," I said.

"Huh? A what now?"

"Come on, David, you heard me. Are you gonna help me or not?"

"Do I even wanna know what happened?" he asked.

"Nah, you really don't."

For a minute, he just looked at me, probably seeing me for the first time, since I was normally viewed as square. But now I was thinking about a murder. If he only knew the half of it.

"Okay, so where is this body?" he asked.

"In the trunk of my car."

"You're bullshittin,' right? Please tell me you ain't ridin' around with a fucking body in your trunk like this is a muh'fuckin' mob movie," he said in disbelief.

"Listen, the shit just happened, and I don't need your judgment. I need your goddamn help!" I replied, getting more frustrated the longer we sat there doing nothing.

"Calm the fuck down and show me the body, nigga," he said, opening his door and getting out.

I did the same and led him to my car, only popping the trunk once he was standing in front of it so no prying eyes would catch a glimpse. When I joined him at the trunk he just stared at me then looked back at the body, and back at me. Without a word, he slammed the trunk and started walking back towards his truck, leaving me no choice except to follow. Once we were back in his truck he still didn't say anything as he took a cigarette from his pack in the console and lit it.

"Was that a cop?" he asked, exhaling a heavy cloud of smoke.

"Yeah!"

"You...shot...a...cop?" he asked slowly.

"I didn't have a choice, David. The situation was out of control."

"Yo, just knowing you right now will get me a life sentence. What the fuck were you thinking?"

The answer to that question was far more complicated than we really had time to answer, and right now there was only one thing on my mind.

"Look, are you gonna help me or not?" I asked.

"You know we family and I love you, but I don't want no parts of this. I can tell you where to go, and if you're smart, you'll put those gas cans to use and send the whole car up in flames."

"And then how do I get home?" I asked. He started to shake his head, but I stopped him.

"All you gotta do is show me where to go, and give me a ride home when done. I'll do everything in between," I bargained.

I could see the hesitation written all over his face, but he still pulled out his phone and made the call I needed. Once that was done I hopped out his truck and got back behind the wheel of my car, following him close so I wouldn't get lost. Within fifteen minutes we pulled up in front of a junkyard in a part of town that I'd never been in. I heard David tap his horn twice and the razor wired gate protecting the entrance rolled back allowing us to drive in. We both got out and were met by a short, bald, black dude wearing faded grease stained coveralls with no shirt underneath to hide his gut or grey chest hair. There was no exchange of words between the man and David. I just watched my cousin hand over a knot of money and the man retreated the way he'd come.

"You owe me two grand by the way," David said coming over to me.

"I got you."

"Okay, so what you're gonna do is pull your car all the way to the back of the junkyard because there's a crusher back there. You're gonna set it on fire and it'll be crushed into something resembling a soda can by sunrise, but take the body out the back first."

"Why?" I asked.

"Because that has to be burned in a separate oil drum and that'll be crushed, too. Don't worry."

"Let's get this over with," I said, going and getting back behind the wheel of my car.

David left his truck parked and hopped in my passenger seat, pointing out where I needed to go and what to do when we got there. I followed instructions, making sure not to leave my guns or the cop's revolver in the car before I covered it in gas and set a match to it. While I was tending to that David was nice enough to make sure the oil drum was ready for the next part. Once the body was stuffed inside and soaked with gas the barbeque began. For the first time in what seemed like hours I finally took a deep breath.

"Do we need to stand here and watch until the fires burn out?" I asked.

"You can if you want, but you'll miss your ride home," he replied, walking back towards where we'd left his truck. I caught up quickly after grabbing the guns.

"I need to dump these real fast," I said once we were back in the truck.

"I got you, cuz, and we gonna stop at an ATM so you can get my money, too."

"I ain't got my wallet on me, but you know I'm good for it fam," I replied.

"Yeah, you good for it...let me drop something on you though, Stephon. This ain't you, bruh. I've known you your whole life and I know you ain't no bitch, but you ain't no killer either."

"I'm not a killer, shit just got out of hand..."

"You think I'm stupid?" he asked, looking straight ahead out the windshield as we pulled through the gate and back out onto the streets.

"What you mean?" I asked.

"I know what's been going on, but we fam, my nigga, and it ain't my place to judge. Plus, I know what it's like when you lose your pops."

The fact that I knew how true those words were kept me from speaking right away. I wouldn't feed him excuses like he didn't understand or know my pain, but I wondered if he'd understand my reasoning.

"They shot him for no reason man. No reason! You knew my dad, David. He wasn't reaching for a gun or anything looking like one."

"I know, I never believed that from the jump. And when that cop turned up dead I was glad because he got what his coward ass deserved, but the rest of it…I mean where does it end?" he asked.

"It'll end when they care about a black man dying as much as they do a white one."

"Come on, Stephon, you know that's not realistic, because people don't change overnight. So are you gonna keep killing white folks for years? Nah, because they're gonna catch you and then you're just another dead body added to the pile," he said, finally looking at me.

"I've been careful…"

"Whatever happened tonight showed that your ass wasn't careful enough! Take it from someone that knows. These streets and all the crimes committed in them got an expiration date, my nigga. Everybody's time runs out, you feel me?"

I gave his words careful consideration, not just because we were family, but because I knew he was really 'bout that life. Did I truly think I could go on killing for the years it would take to undo what had been done? If so, what kind of monster did that make me because to even embark on that journey took the appetite of a serial killer. I didn't consider myself to be that type of person. I simply wanted my life and the life of my children to mean more than some statistics.

We rode on in silence, stopping only long enough for me to wipe the guns off and add them to the collection in the Potomac. I knew I had a lot to think about and as crazy as it seemed I was still very undecided about what I was gonna do. The street life wasn't my life, but what parent wouldn't sacrifice so their child could live better than they did?

ASAD

"A bruh, I really appreciate you being there for me tonight," I said once we'd come to a stop behind my house.

"You know I got you, my nig, but you really need to think about what I'm saying. A revolution is needed, true indeed, but it's other ways to go about it. I wanna stand behind you, not stand over you. Hear me?"

"Yeah, I hear you, bruh, and I love you," I replied truthfully.

"Cool. Show me that love when you bring me my money tomorrow, because I'm telling you now, nigga, don't make me come back over here," he said laughing.

"I got you," I told him, climbing from the truck and making my way through my backyard.

As quietly as I could, I let myself back in the house and reset the alarm. It was already four a.m., which meant there was no need to even think about sleep. I put a pot of coffee on and hit it for my room so I could take a shower. Thankfully, Melody was still fast asleep, and I moved like a ninja straight towards my closet where I got undressed and grabbed a towel.

"I know what you've been up to," Melanie said when I came out of the closet, her voice caused me to visibly jump.

When I went in to get undressed she'd been lying down, but now she was sitting up with her back against the wall, her blue eyes glowing like sapphires in the night.

"Wh…what are you talking about, baby?" I asked, hoping my voice didn't sound as shaky as it felt.

"You know what the fuck I'm talking about, Stephon, I'm not stupid. I know it's you. I know you're the killer on the highway."

104

CHAPTER TWELVE

Her words froze me. It felt like all the blood in my veins had stopped flowing the moment she spoke my truth aloud. I knew somewhere down the line this conversation would take place, but I hadn't expected it to be so soon. In my opinion, I'd been more than careful, so I didn't understand how my wife was now making the statement with a look of absolute certainty on her face. Unless it was a bluff.

"Baby, I don't know what you're talking about," I said walking towards her and grabbing her by her arm.

"Ow! Stephon, you're hurting me."

I loosened my grip a little, but still I pulled her from the bed and led her across the hall into the bathroom. Only when the door was closed and the shower was running did I speak again.

"What the fuck is going on?" I asked.

"You know damn well what's going on. Don't lie to me."

"Okay, first of all, if you actually believed what you just said in there why would you say it in there?" I asked, feeling the beginnings of panic creep up my spine.

"What, do you think I have got a microphone in my coochie? I had a lapse in judgment, but it's not everyday a wife discovers her husband is a goddamn serial killer!" She yelled in a fierce whisper.

"I'm not a serial killer!" I replied empathetically and in the same tone of voice.

"If you kill more than three people that's what they call you, and you're way past three!"

"Goddammit, Melody, don't you understand?" I said, throwing my hands up in frustration.

"Understand? *Understand?* You want me to understand this shit like there is some rational explanation to justify what you've done?" she asked in disbelief.

The fear I felt when she asked me that question was sobering. The consequences for what I did had crossed my mind before, but I'd never envisioned that losing her could be one of the things to happen. The way she was coming at me put a spotlight on that possibility.

"Baby, please, just hear me out for a minute," I pleaded, sitting down on the toilet, and taking her hands to greet her right in front of me. I could feel the tension in her body, but she didn't pull away. Her eyes didn't look like she'd closed herself off from hearing me.

"I won't make excuses, because I know what I've done is wrong by any definition of the word, but I did wrong for the right reasons. The world may never know or appreciate my father's life, but I do and I carry that with me every single day. All of these years we stood up in school to say the Pledge of Allegiance I did with a sense of pride and I believed those words. Even as more and more shootings of unarmed black men happened I still held on to the hope that eventually the broken system would get it right. But the moment my father was executed right next to me, I knew they wouldn't. Even before my police interview turned into an interrogation, and the DA refused to file charges, I understood my dad was gonna be seen as another nigger of circumstances that wouldn't change, because only certain people cared. So, then my fears became reality. I knew that experience was the best teacher, and mainstream America wouldn't get it until it was their blood seeping into the cracks in the pavement. I wanted them to know and relate to the costs every black person pays for the supposed freedom we were given, because that's shit ain't free."

"Stephon... I know what happened to your dad wasn't right and I know how devastating that loss has been for you, but how does becoming what you have fix anything? Yes, you've managed to change the conversation for the moment and show the blatant contrast between black and white. But you've also managed to put this country on edge and in the throes of racial division that hasn't been seen since the fifties and sixties. People are mad, baby...."

"And they should be, that's the point! It's been too many years of our voices, our lives, and contributions not mattering," I said passionately.

"So you want a war, is that it?"

"I want my child to be more than just another nameless, faceless nigger," I replied.

"And I want my child to be more than the statistic you're going to make him by not being around to raise him. You want to change the world, but think of how much your child's world changes if you ain't in it," she said with tears in her eyes.

The truth in that statement left me speechless for a moment. I couldn't imagine growing up without my dad. I mean he'd been my best friend. I'd learned so much, not just from what he said, but from the way he carried himself. He didn't have to tell me how to treat a woman because he showed me how by keeping a smile on my mom's face. He didn't have to tell me the benefits of hard work, because he showed me by being a man that always provided for his family. I couldn't imagine not being that and more for my child someday. I pulled Melody into my arms and put my head against her stomach. Right now my little boy or girl was safe, but soon he or she would be born into chaos, into cruelty beyond comprehension. It was my job to keep my little one safe.

"I feel lost, Mel. This life we're getting ready to bring into the world is in our hands, it's our responsibility, baby, but there are many things beyond our control. Things have got to change and I feel like to act any different only makes me a house nigger instead of a worker in the field."

"Baby, I can't speak to what it's like being black or mistreated for that reason alone. But as a woman who loves her black man and as the mother of a mixed child, I will always stand up for change and equality. We can't do it this way though," she said rubbing my head gently.

"So then how?"

"I don't know, but I know that any real change will take time and if you're going to be here to see that change then you have to stop," she insisted.

Deep down I knew I had to accept the truth of this, but I wouldn't stop trying to find a way to affect change. I owed my dad that much.

"Do you still love me?" I asked, leaning back so I could look up into her eyes.

"For better or for worse, babe, but you've got to promised me that this shit stops now."

"I promise... But there is something you should know," I replied hesitantly.

I pulled her onto my lap and whispered in her ear all that had transpired from the time I left last night until I'd gotten back this morning. Certain parts of the story caused her to shiver, but she kept her poker face and her emotions to herself.

"Am I gonna have to handcuff you to me before I go to sleep?" she asked seriously.

"No, babe, but I do have a question. How did you know?"

"Well, for one, being pregnant means I use the bathroom frequently in the middle of the night. After what happened the first time I caught you missing I couldn't write it off as just one accident when I woke up and you were gone. Plus, I remembered you vaguely mentioning some plan of yours."

"I see. I'm sorry I kept it from you and..."

"Don't be sorry. Just don't do it again," she said slapping me upside my head.

108

I knew that was the least I deserved. Besides, I didn't know one woman who could know what she knew about me and still stand by my side. That was love on another level for real.

"Can I have a kiss?" I asked, giving her my best puppy dog smile.

"Baby, I love you, but if you think you're anywhere near out of the doghouse, then you don't know me at all," she replied, getting up off my lap and stepping into the shower.

I didn't think she was serious until I attempted to join her and I was told in no uncertain terms to get the fuck out. I hated to be at odds with her, but given the situation I felt that the least I could do was respect that she needed time. I waited until she finished taking her shower and then I got in. The hot water didn't wash away all my problems, but I did feel like a weight was lifted off of me, simply because the one person I trusted the most knew my darkest secrets. Despite the love between us, part of me had always expected her to leave once she found out the truth.

I was never happier than to be wrong, and I thank God for my woman. Finishing up my shower, I decided to take the day off because I had some making up to do. Melody deserved a vacation, and now seemed like the perfect time, before she was too big to fly. Plus, getting out of town seemed like a smart move for me. After drying off and putting on some jeans and a t-shirt, I called Ms. Jacobs and told her to clear both mine and Melody's schedule for the next two weeks. I wanted to take her somewhere nice, and preferably outside of the US. Somewhere they couldn't send for me should my name come up in their investigation. With the obstacle of work taken care of, I went in search of my wife.

"Melody, baby, I got a surprise for..."

I pulled up short at the sight of her and my mom sitting at the kitchen table, tears shining brightly in my mother's eyes. I hadn't told Melody not to say shit to mom, but I didn't think I had to because she should've known how that would affect her.

"Stephon, baby, you need to sit down for a minute," Melody said to me.

I'd only seen my mother's face because my wife had her back to me, but as I made a move to go towards my mom I caught Melody's profile. Her cheeks were wet with tears too. This gave me a bad feeling because it was becoming quickly apparent that whatever this was wasn't about me.

"What's wrong, Mama?" I asked, sitting in the chair on the other side of her.

"I...I just got a call from Rita," she said, wiping the tears from her face, but still not turning to look at me.

Rita was my cousin David's mom, and hearing her name made me think of the conversation I just had with David a few hours ago when he told me that everything on the streets had an expiration date. I prayed that conversation wasn't his moment of clairvoyance.

"What happened?" I asked, raising myself as best I could.

"David was on his way home and h...he got pulled over off of South Capitol Street on the Maryland side and...and he got shot," my mom stated softly.

I closed my eyes, picturing my cousin as I'd just seen him a little while ago, finding it hard to believe how quickly shit went bad. The weight of guilt was instantaneous as I accepted the fact that once again someone I love and cared about was shot because of me. Being with me till the early morning hours had changed David's whole schedule, and had he not been there with me he wouldn't have been shot. I was familiar with the area were my mom said it went down, so I knew the cops out that way were from Prince George's County. Ruthless muh'fuckas. I could be ruthless too though.

"Who was the cop that killed him?" I asked, opening my eyes to find my wife staring at me. Behind the tears I could see the plea in her eyes and it hurt my heart to know that I couldn't give her what she wanted. Blood cry for blood.

"He's not dead," my mom said, turning to look at me.

"Huh?"

"He is not dead. He got hit twice, but still managed to pull off in his truck and get away from the cop who shot him. Right now he is at Greater Southeast Hospital."

"Thank God," I murmured, feeling a relief that was indescribable, because another loved one's life hadn't been taken. But I couldn't deny the pressure I still felt to act because the situation as a whole was more of the same, and it needed to stop.

"How's Aunt Rita holding up?" I asked.

"She is fine, she's at the hospital with David and that's why she called," my mom said.

"What do you mean?"

"David was to see you," she said.

In a way this surprised me, but not as much as it would've a few weeks ago. David and I had established new boundaries of trust, and knowing him he needed me to handle something with regards to his business endeavors.

"I'll go see him now," I said standing up.

"I'm going with you," Melody said quickly.

"Mom, will you be okay?"

"I'm fine. You two be safe."

ASAD

CHAPTER THIRTEEN

"What's wrong, Melody?" I asked.

"What do you mean?"

"I mean you're acting weird and you have been since before we left the house."

"I'm fine, Stephon," she replied, still looking out the window at the city alive with the morning hustle and bustle of rush hour. She'd been quiet the whole ride, but I couldn't really put my finger on her mood.

"Do you want to get something to eat?" I asked.

"No."

That one word answer told me that so much was wrong, because pregnant women didn't refuse food. That was almost sacrilegious. I did still have one ace up my sleeve that would, hopefully, put a smile back on her face.

"Listen, sweetheart, I know I have a lot to do in order to make up for what I've done, but everything starts with us. You and I are the foundation that everything is built on, so in order for us to begin working on some things I thought we should take a trip."

"A trip? A trip where?" she asked with more disinterest than I had expected.

"Wherever you want to go, babe. I've cleared our schedule for two weeks and all we gotta do is pick the destination."

"That's not going to fix it, Stephon. I saw the look in your eyes," she said, turning to look at me.

"What do you want me to say, my cousin just got shot," I replied defensively.

"I know that, and I'm sorry that it happened. But that doesn't give you the right to retaliate."

I let that statement hang in the air, choosing not to engage in a discussion where someone could be listening or where I'd be

forced to lie. Muh'fucka tried to body my cousin. Was I just supposed to let that slide? Thankfully, we were at the hospital so I
could avoid this conversation for now. I knew it wouldn't go under the radar forever, Melody wasn't timid or afraid to speak her
mind, and on this subject, she damn sure meant to be heard. I
parked my car and we went in through the emergency room entrance. I hated the smell of hospitals. Even though I hadn't been
shot when my dad was, I still had to go to the hospital to get
checked out. Now every time I caught a whiff of bleach and death
it took me back to that night.

"I need to know what room David Harris is in," I said to the
nurse sitting behind the ER desk.

"One moment while I check that for you... Okay, he is in
room 104, that's right down the hall second door on your right,"
she replied.

I took Melody's hand and we followed the directions given,
not bothering to knock once we got there, but walked straight in
the room. The first bed was unoccupied, but I could see David
lying flat on his back in the second bed hooked up to a number
of beeping machines and it froze me in place. To me, David had
always been larger-than-life and invincible to the shit normal
people fell victim to. He was a gangsta and he was good at it.

But in that moment I didn't see that David, I saw a skinny
kid who looked fragile and unable to fight and the knock of death
at his door. I wasn't sure how to deal with that, and I probably
would have backed out of the room had it not been for Melody.
She gave me a reassuring squeeze that helped strengthen my
spine and put one foot in front of the other until we were standing
at the foot of his bed.

"I'm glad you came so quickly," my Aunt Rita said.

I couldn't remember the last time I'd seen her, but life had
definitely been hard lived since then. Her hair had gone almost
completely white and her skin was starting to sag way from her

face, causing a constant frown, probably because there wasn't much to smile about. She'd always been petite, but it looked like she was hiding in the sweatshirt and jeans she was wearing. The real change was in her eyes though. I could remember those same eyes dancing like Hershey kisses in a commercial because they were so full of life. But now they were tired, making me wonder how much they'd actually seen in a lifetime.

"Of course you know I'd be here, Auntie," I said. At the sound of our voices David opened his eyes and I could tell right away that he was on some good dope. "How you holding up, cuzzo?"

"Take more than some piece of shit cop to kill me, bruh," he replied, his voice coming out stronger than I'd expected.

"True. Tell me what happened, bruh," I said.

"Man, I just hit the drive through at Mike's Liquor Store in Oxen Hill to grab me a bottle before I went to the crib when this cop got behind me flashing his lights."

"So what did you do?" I asked.

"I took my time pulling over, you know try to clean some shit up, but eventually I got over to the side of the road. Dude comes up and asked for my license and registration so I go in the glove box to get it and when I turned back around he's reaching for his pistol.

"Why would he do that, didn't he tell you to go in the glove compartment and get it?" I asked.

"Yeah, but I don't know... See he said that he saw my gun, but I knew my shirt was over it so..."

"Wait, back up. What are you talking about?" I asked, not liking how this was sounding.

"My gun was in my lap under my shirt, just in case he tried to shake, and I was right. He said he saw my gun, but that's bull-shit as I didn't reach for it until..."

"My nigga, you actually reached for your gun?" I asked in disbelief.

"He had his pointing at me, what the fuck was I supposed to do?" he asked like he really believed he did the right thing.

"So then what happened?" I asked.

"I managed to squeeze off one round through my door before I met with two in the chest. I threw my truck in gear and sped off, but I ended up passing out and smashing into something, and then I woke up here," he concluded.

As mad as I was that he'd gotten shot, I knew just from his version of events that shit could've been way worse. If the cop truly did see David's pistol, then he's lucky the muh'fucka didn't dome check him instead of putting two in his chest.

"Did your shot hit the cop?" I asked.

"I wish. Muh'fuckas already been in here talk about charging me with attempted capital murder."

Even with me being a novice in all the workings of the criminal justice system, I knew the way that sounded it was about to get ugly. The look on my aunt's face said she understood the same thing.

"Damn, bruh," I said shaking my head.

"Ay, Mom, why don't you go get something to eat so I can holler at Stephon really quick," he said, using the buttons on the remote in the bed to slowly adjust himself into a semi-sitting position.

"I'll go with you," Melody offered, giving my hand one final squeeze before letting go. Before this time, Melody had been standing silently by my side taking it all in.

My aunt didn't say anything. She simply got up and followed Melody from the room. Her life was on autopilot.

"Your mom okay?" I asked.

"Yes, she'll be straight. She just worries too much."

"Only because she loves you though."

"I know... Which is why I need your help."

"What do you need?"

"You know what I need," he replied, staring at me intently.

"I don't understand."

"Yes, you do. This muh'fucka shot me, cuz. Tried to raise me from the world like I wasn't shit. And now that he didn't succeed he's trying to bring a case against me that could have me doing thirty years minimum! You know what I need you to do," he said nodding his head.

I understood exactly what he was saying. He wanted me to kill the cop that had tried to kill him, which didn't seem like an unreasonable request given what we'd gone through this morning. The problem was that there was an obstacle standing between me and ending this cop's life. My conscience. From the way David told his story it sounded like the cop had just been doing his job, which meant he was one of the good guys.

"Let me ask you something, why did he pull you over anyway?"

"He said he followed me coming out of Barry Farms because it was a big drug area. I know he didn't see me making no sales though, so he shouldn't have fucked with me."

David was probably right and the cop may not have seen him make any sales this time, but how many times had he seen David in the neighborhood doing shit he had no business doing? Had he ever overlooked something or let something slide in hopes that David would get his shit together? I didn't know the answer to that any more than I knew the cop's story from last night. I'd killed him out of survival, and if I was completely honest with myself that shit didn't set well with me even now. So how was I going to kill another cop for simply doing his job?

"Ay bruh, I don't know if that's the best course of action," I said.

"Fuck you mean?" he replied, more than a little hostile.

"I mean that's not really a smart move at the moment because shit is hot right now and..."

"And who made shit hot, my nigga? Who got the whole damn country on high alert like Osama bin Laden is back from the dead? Don't talk to me about hot shit, and don't act like I didn't help your ass when you needed me. This time I need you."

A thick silence hung between us as I tried to digest his words while trying to formulate a response in my mind. He was right, he had helped me when I needed him most and so it would be fucked up for me to turn my back on him now. I can admit that. But what I didn't like was the threat that I saw in his eyes. Maybe I was overthinking or maybe I was simply paranoid from all that had taken place, but to me his eyes held the threat of exposure and he was trying to mask it with defiance at the thought of me not helping.

I felt bad for even thinking what I was in that moment because this was my cousin, my blood, and that meant I should trust him without reservation. At the same time, on the other side of that coin was the thirty years he mentioned he'd be looking at. Today's motto regarding the street life was *why do ten when you could tell on a friend,* so did I really expect him to stand up under thirty?

"What exactly do you want done?"

"I want him gone."

"Okay, but that won't stop the courts from taking you to trial, bruh."

"No, but it will be my word against his and he won't be able to speak for himself," he reasoned with a smile on his face.

The more he talked I swear the more my bad feeling about this whole thing increased. Maybe it was that good dope they shot him up with that had him missing the bigger picture, because if he thought his word was more powerful than he did a cop's, he had life locked up. The sad thing was that I didn't see a lot of options for myself.

"What's the cop's name?" I asked reluctantly.

"James Hudson."

"What am I supposed to do about weapons?"

"My mom will give you the keys to my place here in the city, it's a stash spot. There's a safe under the floorboards by the front door and there is a button on my key ring that opens the floorboards, but you've gotta be standing right on top of it when you hit the button. The combo is 2-21-07 and you'll find what you need inside," he replied.

"What's the address?"

He rattled off some apartment building over on Southwest not too far from where we were, which meant I could go there once we left.

"Aight, I got you."

"Don't fuck this up, Stephon, I'm serious. Oh, and you can keep that two G's you owe me and just consider it a fee-for-rush delivery on this."

"Baby, I got you a breakfast burrito," Melody said coming into the room ahead of my aunt.

"Thanks, baby, I'll eat it on the way out."

"We're leaving?" she asked handing me my food.

"Yeah. Auntie I need David's keys," I said, avoiding the questioning look Melody was trying to drill into my skull. My aunt gave me the keys and I kissed her on the cheek before heading for the door.

"Be safe, cuzzo," David called from behind me.

I gave him a thumbs-up without turning around and held the door for Melody as we made our exit. As soon as we were back in the hallway, I started eating my sausage, egg, and cheese burrito in hopes of discouraging conversation. I knew my wife was going to have questions, but I didn't have the answer she wanted to hear right now, so it was best not to talk. Besides, answering to her wasn't my biggest problem of the moment. I had to figure out what the fuck my next move was going to be. To kill or not to kill? When the fuck did that become the question of the day in my life? I felt like I was living someone else's story with no way of knowing what the ending would be.

"That must have been some conversation you and David had," Melody commented once we were back in the car. It was obvious she was setting the bait for me, but I didn't take it.

"I am just glad he's alive, because shit could've gone way different," I said.

"I know. What the hell was he thinking anyway reaching for a gun, especially with all this shit going on in the world today? He could've easily been a justifiable homicide."

"He probably figured that cops shoot people like him anyway, so it's better to go down fighting," I replied, starting the car and pulling out of the parking lot.

I was having my doubts about taking Melody along with me to the apartment, but I didn't see how to avoid it without a lot of questions. There were going to be questions any way I sliced it, the biggest one of all being whether or not I told her the truth.

"Do you feel the same way he does?" she asked.

"What do you mean?"

"I mean are you going to start riding around with a pistol on your lap in case you get pulled over? Keep in mind that not all cops are crooked," she stated matter-of-factly.

"I know they're all not crooked, Mel, and no I won't be riding around like that. Give me some credit, I do have a little bit of sense."

"Very little," she said under her breath.

I chose to ignore her comment instead of feeding into it, keeping my eyes on my surroundings in an effort not to get lost.

To Die In Vain

"Where are we going?" she asked, obviously noticing that we weren't heading home.

"I gotta stop by David's house real quick."

"I thought he lived in Maryland," she said.

"He does, but he has apartments around the city."

"Okay, and why would you be going to one of these apartments?"

"Because I gotta pick something up," I replied vaguely.

"Stephon."

I turned to look at her briefly wondering what look I would find on her face. Sure enough, she was giving me the look that said I better stop making her ask more questions than necessary.

"Shit is so complicated right now, can we please not do the third-degree thing?" I asked.

"It doesn't have to be a third-degree thing if you just tell me what the hell is going on."

"What's going on is I have no choices! I've gotta kill that cop."

ASAD

CHAPTER FOURTEEN

"I'm sorry would you like to run that past me one more goddamn time," Melody said calmly.

I didn't want to repeat myself. I didn't want to have a conversation that I knew would ultimately hurt the woman that I loved more than life. But life wasn't about only what I wanted. I waited until I pulled up in front of the building and gathered my thoughts before I answered.

"David wants the cop gone," I said.

"Tell me why that's your problem."

"Because as he not so subtly reminded me, he helped me when I needed him."

"Okay, but baby, that was destroying evidence. That was not doing some shit that could get you lethally injected!" she replied, raising her voice in frustration.

"I swear to you, it's the last time and..."

"No! You know, Stephon, there is no one more time shit. You've managed to get away with all the twisted shit you've done and I'm not about to let you press your luck because your cousin made a dumb ass mistake," she ranted.

I waited until she ran out of words for the moment, until she was trying to catch her breath from all the expended energy, before I reached for her hand. I felt the tremble in her fingertips, but still the warmth of her palm against mine gave me comfort. I needed both her comfort and her strength if I had any hope of getting through whatever was coming next. First, I had to make her understand.

"Baby, I need you to listen to me for a second please. I have to do this because if I don't David is gonna trade my life for his when his day in court comes."

"Did...did he actually say that to you?" she whispered.

ASAD

The fear dancing in her big blue eyes broke my heart, because
I knew no matter what position David put me in it was still my
fault for allowing it to happen.

"He didn't have to say it, I saw it all over his face," I replied
sadly.

"But...but...that's your cousin, your family. And given his
lifestyle he knows you'd be looking at the death penalty if con-
victed. Are you telling me none of that matters?"

"No," I said, hating myself more as tears spilled onto her
cheeks. Her eyes had seen too many tears because of me.

"Baby, please don't cry, I'm going to fix this I promise," I
said, wiping her tears away and giving her a soft, tender kiss. "Sit
right here. I'll be right back."

"No, I'm coming you," she said, gripping my hand tighter.

"Okay, but you're going to have to let my hand go so we can
get out."

Reluctantly, she let my hand go, but once we were on the
sidewalk in front of the building she had my hand clutched in
hers again. We made our way into the rundown building up to the
third floor. I opened the door and let us in, then made sure we
were locked in before I moved the rug in front of the door.

"What are you doing?" she asked.

"Just hold on and you'll see."

Holding my hand directly over where the rug had been I
pressed the button attached to the key ring and watched in amaze-
ment as the floor dropped and pushed back revealing a safe.

"Damn, is your cousin 007?"

"Nah, he's a dope boy," I said, kneeling down and punching
in the combination before turning the knob to open the safe.

The first thing I saw was the darkness at the end of the gun
barrel staring up at me. I reached in and pulled a Taurus 9 mm
out, sitting it next to me while I inspected the rest of the contents.
There were a couple of platinum chains, about $100,000 in cash,

a pound of weed, and a Mac-90 submachine gun with an extra clip.

"What did he send you here to get?"

"A pistol."

"That's a lot of money," Melody said, coming to stand right beside me.

I wasn't paying attention to that, I was busy inspecting the 9 mm to make sure it was locked and loaded. With that done, I started putting everything back in the safe.

"Stephon," she said, kneeling beside me and grabbing my arm.

"What, babe?"

"We could leave," she said taking his stacks of money back out of the safe.

"What?"

"You said it yourself, we need a vacation, but with this money we can lay low for a while."

"How long is a while?" I asked.

"Until shit blows over with David, I guess. I don't know." I could see the wheels in her head turning behind her eyes, but it was obvious she forgot one crucial fact.

"Sweetheart, there's no statute of limitations on murder," I said softly.

The way her shoulders slumped in defeat made me want to cry, but now wasn't the time to give her false hope. We had to live in the truth.

"So then we just stay on the run," she said.

"Can you really do that, babe? That would mean never seeing your family again and them never seeing the baby. And can you imagine how hard life could be trying to survive on the run with a baby?"

"I can imagine how hard life would be trying to survive without you...I'd rather run than live that way," she replied earnestly.

I knew she meant what she was saying, but I couldn't ask her to do that, not even for what we had. This was my mess and my bed to lie in because of the decisions I'd made.

"We gotta go, babe," I said softly, taking the money out of her hands and putting it in the safe with everything else before I closed it. I didn't even have to press the button for the floor to pop back into place.

I tucked the gun in my pants, unlocked the door and ushered Melody out, before relocking the door behind us. We were quiet all the way back to the car, and the ride home was filled with more of the same strained silence. I didn't know what I was supposed to say, because no words could make the situation better. It was evident that both of us had a really bad feeling about what my next move would be, but we both understood that alternative options were nonexistent. Neither of us attempted to get out of the car when I pulled into the garage.

"What if you..."

"What, sweetheart?" I asked.

"What if you got rid of your cousin instead?"

"I can't do that, baby, he's family."

"Family that's willing to sell your ass up the river if you don't do what he wants," she said frustrated.

I couldn't argue with the truth of what she was saying, but he was still family. Unwilling to debate this point I got out of my car and went into the house.

"How's your cousin holding up?" my mom asked when I walked into the living room. The fact that she was sitting in the living room staring at a TV that wasn't on didn't escape my notice as I took a seat on the couch beside her.

"He's okay, I guess. Full of that good hospital medication," I replied somberly.

"And Rita?"

"Aunt Rita is...holding on I guess is the best way to describe it. To be honest she looks drained, but I understand the enormous amount of stress she must feel."

"I can definitely relate." My mom still hadn't made eye contact with me, and even though she physically resembled her normal self, I could tell by her voice that she was off, or she would have noticed my own emotional distress.

"What's wrong, Mom? Talk to me." I heard Melody come in through the garage door of the kitchen, but her footsteps echoed in the direction of our bedroom.

"I'm just tired, Stephon."

"Why don't you get some rest then?" I asked.

"Not that kind of tired, son. I'm tired of all the bullshit life throws at me. I'm tired of my family being hurt or affected by violence. I'm tired of history's repetition when it comes to how black people are treated, and how black people don't make it easy on themselves by doing dumb shit. I don't even know the story when it comes to what happened with David, but I know if he didn't live his life a certain way he wouldn't make such an easy target," she said sincerely.

I had never heard my mom voice herself like this before. Not that she was quiet, easy, or without an opinion, but these conversations normally took place between her and my dad. It was plain to see that she missed him a lot.

"The way you feel is understandable, Mom, but you have to trust that things will get better."

"How? By killing white folks? That shit is dumb on a whole different level."

"What do you mean?" I asked.

"I know you feel like some others do who say those random killings made white people feel what we felt, but that's not all it's about. Black people deserve equality and the only way to get that is to let your voice be heard. Do you think anyone can hear the lasting message over their fear?" she asked.

"I don't know."

"This country was molded on the arrogance that white people are somehow better than anyone else, and the only thing I've seen that will dissuade that opinion is when someone shows them how wrong they are. Killing them means we can do what they do, but it doesn't make us better or equal. Showing them that we can overcome what they do, and thrive instead of just survive, forces them to swallow that hard reality they've been trying to avoid.

"You can't write history without us in it, so if we can change the world because we've done it before, but if we're just gonna resort to killing then everything we've ever done was done in vain. I refuse to believe my husband died in vain," she said, shaking her head.

I'd never had shit broken down to me as if she'd known what I'd been doing, but really she was just a black woman who was old enough to have seen the world change. Hearing the passion in her voice made me want to believe in what she said, but I'd be lying if I said I wasn't skeptical. Was it the impatience of my generation that prevented me from seeing a future that wasn't shaped by the fear and respect violence inspired? Or was it my refusal to admit that I was part of the problem instead of the solution? One thing I did know was that my mom had given me a hell of a lot to think about.

"Dad didn't die in vain, Mom, and he'll be remembered and mourned forever," I said, reaching for her hand and giving it a reassuring squeeze before I got up off the couch.

Something in me knew that she wanted to be alone with her thoughts, and I needed to be with my wife to discuss hers. I knew there was no way to convince her to think like me, but I had to try and provide her with some type of comfort. I knew she was distressed and it was completely my fault. Taking a deep breath

I stilled myself and mentally prepared for what I was going to say, but when I walked into our room those words got lost in my throat. Before me was the most beautiful sight I'd ever seen, and I never tired of seeing it wearing nothing except a smile. I found Melody laying flat on her back, motioning me toward her with one finger.

"Uh, what's going on, baby?" I asked, closing and locking the bedroom door behind me before I started my journey in her direction.

"Come closer and you'll find out," she said seductively.

Just the sound of her voice had the hairs on the back of my neck standing at attention, and the rest of me was definitely responding to the visual image of her. I tried to maintain my composure though, so things wouldn't be over before they began.

"You're beautiful, baby," I said, coming to stand before her at the foot of our bed.

"I'm glad you know that, now take off your clothes off for me. Slowly," she ordered.

For a second I hesitated, wondering if she thought amazing sex was going to somehow change my mind about what had to happen. I didn't see the point in asking that question though. I did as I was told, removing one piece of clothing at a time until she and I had matching outfits.

"Now what?" I asked.

"Do you love me, Stephon?"

"You know I love you, babe."

"Do you really love me?" she asked, slowly spreading her legs open.

"Yes, baby."

"I want you to show me then."

On my hands and knees I crawled up there until I was close enough to speak with my tongue. And so began the demonstration of my love for her. Without giving voice to our fears, we still understood the future and its uncertainty, so in that moment we took our time. I never felt more connected to anything or anyone as I did to Melody. With each caress and sigh of ecstatic pleasure a new memory was born. The relevance of time to space didn't matter, nothing mattered except what we were sharing. And share we did.

The world outside may not have had a good understanding of the word equal, but we definitely defined and redefined it in terms of pleasing one another. Again and again we took the journey from Earth to what lay beyond our ability to think in a coherent way. Before I knew it we were surrounded by the shadows of nightfall.

"Are you hungry?" I asked after our latest round of lovemaking.

"I think my stomach is full."

"You're so nasty," I replied laughing.

"I know, but you love me and that's all that matters. Now if you feel the need to continue showing me how much you love me you can cook me dinner."

"I think I can manage that, but I might need some help."

"Just try to get me away from your side," she said kissing me hard on the lips.

We both got out of bed and threw on some clothes before heading for the kitchen. We spent the next hour making homemade burgers and fries like we used to do when we were too young to date without our parent's supervision. It may not have been an expensive meal, but we were rich with memories of days spent together like this. Maybe we were both using the past to avoid the future, but it is what we needed at the moment and I embraced it without hesitation.

"You're the love of my life, you know that," I said once we were sitting at the table across from each other.

At first she didn't answer me, she just stared at me with her heart in her eyes. There was so much love inside her and I felt more than special that it was all for me. Still, the fact of what was to come remained on my mind.

"I know I'm the love of your life, and you're mine," she finally said.

"I can't put into words how sorry I am, sweetheart."

"I...I know, Stephon. And no matter what happens, I know your love for me is real. I'll never question or doubt that. I won't lie to you though. I'm terrified. I don't know how to be without you, but I don't know how to accept what has to be done."

"I never wanted to put you in this situation, Melody," I said, reaching for her hand. Part of me wanted to regret my decisions, but something in me wouldn't let that happen. The situation was impossible, yet filled with so much love for my family and my newly extended family that I couldn't see how I wouldn't make the same decisions all over again.

We ate the rest of our meal holding hands, but not speaking, because we both knew the words in each other's heart. When the food was gone I led my wife back to our bedroom where I made love to her again so tenderly that we both shed tears. I promised her I wouldn't vanish in the night as she found the peace of sleep in my arms. I held her close, savoring the smell of me on her skin and the feel of her heartbeat against my chest. Love was in my arms and in my heart...but in my mind dark thoughts swirled. Death was coming.

ASAD

CHAPTER FIFTEEN

72 Hours Later

I may have wrestled with my conscience about the things I'd done and would have to do, but there was no indecision. When I went back to the hospital to see David and found him handcuffed to his bed, I saw the desperation on his face. And just below the desperation was the not so thinly veiled threat I caught a glimpse of the other day. It was crazy to me that this was the same guy who'd been lecturing me about the shit I was doing and telling me about expiration dates in the streets. He knew all the answers and the street code, but living the consequences of that life wasn't something he wanted to know firsthand.

I could call him weak, but then how should I be viewing myself considering that I was getting ready to kill to avoid those same consequences. Say what you will, but prison seemed worse than death from the outside looking in. At least you could only die once. Even before David started hitting me with twenty questions, I knew there was no turning back, which made it a good thing that I started my research right away. I went about it pretty much the same as I had with that cop that killed my father, checking all social media sites first. Immediately, I found things that made the situation harder, namely the fact that the cop was married and he had two teenage daughters.

Seeing his family pictures and the obvious love they all had for each other made what I had to do tough, but not impossible. I had to force myself not to see any of them as human beings, which made me feel like an animal inside. The only way I was able to keep a straight face was because of the mantra running through my head telling me it was him or me. My wife needed her husband, my child needed his father, and my mother needed her son. Enough said. After I found out about him having a family, I figured the easiest way to get to him was to go through his daughters. Having a cop for a father guaranteed he kept close tabs on them, which meant wherever they were he wouldn't be far behind.

By day two I was using police tactics and pulling stakeouts wherever one of his daughters posted that they would be, and it wasn't that hard given that we were all the same age. Unlike most of my peers though, I didn't feel the need to post every single thing on my Instagram page, but his daughters did. Ultimately, this led me to be where I was now, at Howard University partying like I had been enrolled for years and couldn't wait to graduate. Howard may have been described as a black college, but these two white girls blended in seamlessly and almost lost me a couple of times. It was a safe bet that their dad didn't know they were here, and I was hoping that they wouldn't be here long because they were my ticket to get into their house.

After driving past it a few times in a quiet Silver Spring neighborhood, I realized it was definitely someplace you had to be invited into or you drew suspicion. I needed to get in and out without being remembered if I was seen. So the idea of hiding in the trunk of their car seemed genius to me. I just hated the waiting game because I had to pretend like I was there to party and have a good time when I really wanted to be home with my wife. Things were strained between the two of us and it was mainly because when I left the house she never knew if I was coming back. That kind of stress wasn't good for her and the baby, and I felt like shit for inflicting it on her. I knew she'd purposely avoided bad boys all her life for this reason, but I knew the quicker I got this over with the better we would all be.

"Dance with me," the girl said, taking me by the hand and pulling me on to the makeshift dance floor in the living room.

I had no idea whose frat house this was, but there were women everywhere and they weren't shy. I still had my eyes on the cop's kids across the room, as this college girl backed it up on me like we knew each other. Dancing wasn't exactly my thing, but I needed to blend in. Smoking or drinking weren't my ideas of fun, so I had to fake it. When a slow song came on it was evident the whole tempo of the party was changing and I saw one of the girls check her watch just before the lights dimmed.

The girl who'd been grinding on me now turn around to face me and attempted to put her arms around my neck, but it was time to make my move that my pretend partying was over. I made my excuses and tried to seem apologetic before I made my way outside and hauled ass to the black Toyota Camry that would take me to my destination. It was risky to leave my car and steal away in the girl's car, but I needed the advantages of stealth and surprise. When I got to their car I reached in my pocket for the key I'd bought at the junkyard off the same dude who'd aided in the destruction of the last cop. He said it with a master key and it would work on this particular make and model. Four thousand dollars, he better not have been bullshittin.' I put the key in the lock to open the driver side door so I could pop the trunk, but no sooner had I turned the lock is when my luck ran out.

"What are you doing?" she asked, her voice laced with the accusation she had yet to speak.

Coming towards me was the younger girl, about 5'5", weighing about 120 pounds with sandy blond hair. She was probably cute when she wasn't scowling like she was at the moment. Behind her was her big sister standing about 2 inches taller with the same piercing green eyes that were screaming the words 'thief' as she quickly evaluated the situation. If only that were the worst of my sins.

"Can I help you, ladies?" I asked, pulling the car door open to aid in my effort to confuse them.

"Why are you…wait a minute, isn't that our car, Cindy?" The younger girl said turning to her sister for confirmation.

"I…I thought so," Cindy replied, looking around for any other black Toyota Camrys. They'd given me the small window I needed.

"Both of you get in the car now, and please don't try any dumb shit," I said, pointing the gun at the younger girl's stomach and cocking the hammer.

There was no accusation or confusion in either set of green eyes, there was only room for fear. Obviously, their father had taught them the benefits of listening to someone in my position versus theirs, because both girls complied immediately. Cindy got behind the wheel, her sister took shotgun, and I chose the back seat where I could cover both of them.

"Give me your phones," I ordered once we were all seated.

"Ple…Please don't hurt us," the younger girl said, her voice suddenly smaller than it had been when she thought I was stealing her car.

"Just do what I tell you and you'll be fine."

"Please. Let Sarah go and keep me," Cindy bargained.

"That's a noble gesture, but it doesn't work that way. We're all going to the same spot."

"Are…are you going to rape us, because…"

"No, I'm not going to rape you, or hurt you in any kind of way, if you follow my directions," I replied, feeling impatient.

Those girls tossed their phones to me and waited on my next instruction. In my heart I already knew this wasn't going to end well, because they'd seen my face, but giving them false hope would keep them from being hysterical.

"Start the car and let's go," I ordered. Cindy did as she was told and the journey began.

"Where do you want me to go?" Cindy asked.

"Home." My response caused one girl to look at me in the rearview mirror while the other turned around to face me.

"We...we're going home? To our house?" Sarah asked as confused as ever.

"Yeah."

"But...but...but...our dad..." Cindy gave her a sharp elbow to cut off what she was about to say, but I already knew the truth, of course.

"I know your dad is a cop for PG County," I said, looking Cindy directly in the eyes through the rearview mirror.

My statement forced Sarah to turn back around, but I didn't need to see her eyes to know her mind was moving a mile a minute behind them. They may not have known what was going on, but the fact that I wanted to go to their house while already knowing that their father is a cop said one thing. Trouble. We rode on in silence with the tension that was thick enough to choke an army. I didn't know where their minds were, but mine went to Melody again and again. I hadn't told her what my plans were. I just told her I was going out and then I kissed the tears off her cheeks.

I could still taste the salt from them even now and that made me want to get out of this car and run home into her arms. Reality was that I couldn't do that though, no matter how bad I wanted to. It took a little over an hour before we pulled to a stop on the street in front of their house. I could see no movement on the inside, but common sense said no cop would go to sleep without his babies being tucked in.

"Why are you here?" Cindy asked.

They both had been silent the entire ride, occasionally shooting sideway glances at each other, but it was obvious this was the question at the front of their minds.

"I'm here because I have to be," I replied.

"What does that mean?" Sarah asked.

"You'll see. Get out," I said, motioning with the pistol. The car was turned off, we all got out and closed our doors, and started moving towards the house in a single file.

"If you do anything stupid I will shoot you, and that's a promise," I warned as we got closer to the front door.

I was dressed in black cargo pants and a black hoodie, and as we got closer I slid the gun inside the hoodie pocket so it was concealed but still deadly. I could hear Cindy's nerves in the shaking of the key when she went to stick her house key in the lock to open the door. Taking a deep breath I braced myself for what might be waiting on the other side. I didn't even know the layout of the house, so I was really playing everything by ear. Cindy managed to get the door open and in we all walked into a little alcove.

Sarah immediately shut off the alarm, and I was watching her harder than a fiend did their next hit of dope to make sure she didn't send out a SOS signal from where we stood. There was a staircase directly in front of us leading to the second level of the house, to the left was a living room, to the right was his study, and directly past the stairs was the kitchen. It was from this direction that I heard movement.

"I'm in the kitchen, girls." A man's voice called out.

They both turned to look at me and I nodded, pulling the gun out to reiterate my earlier statement about compliance. I noticed picture after picture of them as a family lining the walls of the hallway as we headed towards the kitchen. Every smile was like a physical blow to my stomach, but I fought to separate my emotions from the situation.

"Hey girls, how was the movie…" As soon as he saw me behind his daughters with the gun in my hand I watched his police instincts kick in and assess the situation rapidly.

I was reading him the same way, taking in the six-foot, 220-pound frame, bald head and glasses. He didn't look imposing standing there in his flannel housecoat, but the speed in which his eyes shifted told me not to underestimate him. A mammoth speeding calculation was a man prone to act fast.

"Who are you and what you want?" he asked calmly.

"Who I am doesn't matter, but what I want is justice, officer."

"Well, I believe in justice and the law, so tell me what I can do to help," he replied.

"First, you can tell me where your wife is."

"She is in bed."

"Let's get her," I said.

I saw a look exchange between the two sisters and then between them and him. They were communicating without words and that was starting to piss me off because I didn't understand, and that was dangerous for me.

"I didn't say look around at each other, so move your asses," I said impatiently.

"Please, sh-she has breast cancer and she is so weak," Sarah said.

I hadn't expected that response. My first thought was that she was lying, but when I looked from her eyes to his I saw the truth. I guess there were some things you didn't post about on Twitter. If she didn't see me maybe I wouldn't have to kill her, or at least if I did it would put her out of her misery.

"You don't need my wife or my kids if you came here for me," he said.

"You're probably right, but in your occupation I'm sure you're familiar with the term collateral damage. You probably have a lot of experience in hurting innocent people."

"My dad's a good cop," Sarah said defensively.

"Oh yeah, tell that to the last black man he put in the morgue, or the one he tried to send there a couple days ago," I replied.

"So that's why you're here, because of that drug dealer's shooting," he said.

"Why is he a drug dealer, because he drives a nice truck or owns a few expensive chains? Or because he's black and lives in a neighborhood full of opportunities to advance himself out of poverty by way of the pharmaceutical trade? Not all young black men sell drugs, cop."

"I'm aware of that. And no he's not a dope dealer because of his truck or his environment, but I had my suspicions when fiends rushed him like he was Santa Claus passing out presents. Based on his actions in a neighborhood of light drug activity I pulled him over."

"And shot him," I said raising my gun to match the cop's eye level.

"He had a gun in plain sight, but I wouldn't have shot him if he hadn't reached for it," he said, raising his hands in a placating gesture.

Most people would've heard what he was saying as nothing more than excuses, but the range of the truce was undeniable. From the beginning I had feared that David had put himself in a bad situation, and here I was getting ready to kill an entire family because of that. The tightness in my chest was just one indicator of how wrong I felt about this was.

"I didn't want to shoot him and I definitely didn't want to kill him. If I had, I would have aimed higher because a head shot at that range is unavoidably fatal." I know from personal experience how true that statement was, but it changes nothing. I couldn't let it.

"All you white cops are the same. You kill unarmed or suspicious black men because a nigger's life will always be expendable to you. Today you learn the worth of a righteous, independent, fearless black man. And you learn the consequences of his wrath," I said, flipping the safety off the gun and preparing to shoot.

"Please don't kill my dad!" Sarah yelled, running to stand in front of him. "He's not perfect, but he is a good man and he never would shoot anyone if he didn't have to. Please, please don't kill him," she cried.

"I know you," Cindy said, suddenly diverting my attention.

"What?" I said.

"I…I know you, I mean I've seen you on Instagram and Snap Chat. You were the one who was actually in the car when his father was shot by the cop in Virginia."

I opened my mouth to protest against what she had said, but the light of certainty in her eyes told me that would be useless. It didn't matter though; it wasn't like I could leave witnesses behind after this. Cop killing was capital murder.

"Oh my God, you're right," Sara chimed in.

"I've been trying to figure it out ever since you got us in the car, but it didn't hit me until just now. I watched what you posted after the shooting happened, and after the system failed yet again to get justice for the innocent. I saw you mourn, but loved how you introduced the world to your father that people would note the great man that was lost. I…I felt your pain, which is why I don't understand how you can stand here ready to take our father from us," Cindy said with tears in her eyes.

"He shot my cousin…"

"Your cousin was in the wrong," Cindy replied empathetically.

"My dad's not a bad cop or a dirty cop. He actually took us down to the protest when your dad was killed," Sara informed me.

I could tell by the shaking of the gun in my hand that my emotions were all over the place, and the screams of indecision in my head were getting louder. Part of me wanted to scream at them to stop the lies, but the part of me that knew they were speaking truth kept me silent. In this moment all I really wanted was to do the impossible and turn back the hands of time.

"You put all those photos, and videos out there for the world to know your dad, and I feel like I did get to know him in some way. He wouldn't want you to do this," Cindy said softly.

"I don't have a choice," I replied apologetically.

"There is always a choice," he said, looking me square in the eyes.

I felt like he was staring at my soul and that made me think of all I'd done in the name of justice. Did I really understand the meaning of the word, and if so, how did that translate into what I was doing in this moment? I had to pull this trigger now in order to gain my freedom...but what good was that freedom if I lost myself?

"I...I don't wanna do this," I said softly.

"Then don't do it," Sarah said.

"It's not that easy, there's no way out of this for me."

"What if there was?" Cindy asked taking a step towards me.

"What do you mean?" I asked warily.

"What if you got out the same way you came in, except you only take me with you instead of both of us?"

"Cindy, no..."

"Dad, it's okay. He's not gonna hurt me, and as long as I'm with him you can't call the police or any type of law enforcement. When he's safely away I'll be free to return. What do you say, Stephon?"

The fact that she actually knew my name made me see her for the first time. She hadn't just glossed over the story of my dad's murder, she really had taken the time to get to know us and that meant something.

"You think you can trust me?" I asked.

"If you give me your word on your father's life, then yes," Cindy replied.

Thinking about my father's life and all he'd stood for made me miss him with an ache that would never truly leave. That was not a pain I wanted my own child to feel, but what could I do? The cards were dealt. It was too late to fold.

ASAD

CHAPTER SIXTEEN

"It's me."

"Stephon, where are you?"

"Right now that's not important, what's important is that you listen to me and do exactly what I tell you. I need you to find the jeans I had on the day we went to the hospital and get the keys to David's apartment. Then I need you to go there and get that money out of the safe."

"Baby, you want me to go into that neighborhood in the middle of the night and come out with one hundred-thousand dollars in cash?" Melody asked in disbelief.

"No, I don't want you to, but we don't have a choice. We've gotta run and we gotta do it now," I replied.

The silence coming from her end of the phone following that statement spoke loudly to me. I knew she wanted to ask questions, but in her mind she already knew what happened and what had to happen next if we were gonna be together.

"I'll do it, Stephon. What do I do once I have the money?"

"I want you to meet me at National Airport, so make sure you have both of our passports, but don't worry about packing anything."

"Okay. How long until you meet me there?"

"I'll be there within an hour."

"I'll wait for you. I love you so much, Stephon," she said with tears thick in her voice.

"I love you too, baby. Make sure you take a bag to put the money in and take the gun out of the safe when you leave, in case anything goes wrong. The combination is 2-21-07."

"Got it. Hurry, babe," she said disconnecting our call.

ASAD

I put my phone back in my pocket while trying to quiet the screaming fear inside me. I hated to send my wife into that environment and situation, but time was a luxury we didn't have. Because of my decisions time had run out.

"You don't have to run away."

"Yes, I do."

"No, you don't. I mean we all understand the trauma of what you've been through. If I didn't I never would've offered to go with you. My dad may be a cop, but he's also a man and a father, and that makes him understanding and reasonable. I promise that as long as I go home safe he won't press charges," Cindy assured me.

"I wish it was that simple," I said, looking out the passenger window of her car.

The decision to let her family live meant I had to take mine and run, but at least I wouldn't have more death on my conscience. I'd tried to disassociate my emotions from what had to be done, but the reality was that every life I'd taken was that of a real person and I didn't get to hide from that. It had taken everything in officer James Hudson to trust his daughter and my word that she would be safe, but that was only because they didn't know what all I'd done. For the moment those demons were mine to hold onto.

"It is that simple, but I won't tell you how to live your life. Maybe getting away for a while will help with the grief, and the frustration. I still can't believe charges weren't filed," she said.

I really didn't feel like having this conversation, so I didn't respond. My mind was on what would happen next. And how long I had before shit hit the fan. It had to be at least a couple months before David got to the point in his trial when he had to trade my name for a sentence reduction. All I needed was enough time to get out of the U.S. and then he could sing like Beyonce if he wanted.

"Do you want me to drive straight to the airport?" she asked.
"Nah, I want you to go back to where the party was so we can change cars."

"Change cars, why?"

"Just in case your dad wants to have a friend looking for yours or if he has this one lojacked," I said, checking the side mirror for any signs of pursuit or flashing lights.

"He won't do that, and trust me, he doesn't have a tracker on my car or I'd be in a world of trouble."

"We're still gonna do this my way," I insisted.

I kept an alert look for any sign of the law as we continued on into the night, but I kept my gun out of sight because I didn't want to scare her. I felt like we had an understanding now and she wasn't my hostage as much as she was a woman that lived in fear of experiencing what I had. The threat of violence to her father was a nightmare that she had to live with daily, and we both understood that when his number came up it would hurt beyond words. Once we got back to my car I let her call her dad like I promised she would every hour before putting her behind the wheel of my car so the journey could continue.

I was finally able to breathe a sigh of relief when Melody texted me and said her mission was accomplished. We agreed to meet at the Motel Six by the airport to decide where we were going. But I didn't care as long as we were together.

"This will all be over soon. I know it probably doesn't count for shit, but I'm sorry I dragged you into all this. Tell your sister that when you get home," I said.

"I'll tell her, but can I ask you a question?"

"I can't promise to answer, but go ahead," I replied, turning so I could see her profile in the glow of the passing street lights.

"Like I said, I follow you on Instagram and Snap Chat, and this doesn't seem like you. Nothing my dad said about your cousin surprised you, and you didn't think he was lying or you would've killed him anyway. So why were you gonna do it in the first place? Do you hate all cops now?"

"No, I don't hate all cops, only the crooked ones."

"You had to have at least thought your cousin might've been in the wrong. Why would you kill for no reason?" she asked genuinely.

Part of me wanted to tell her that this wasn't me, but I was starting to wonder how much of that was true. My mother's words echoed through my brain, making me question the decisions I made, even the ones I justified. Nothing I did seemed to make sense anymore, even when I reminded myself that white people weren't seeing us as equal so I had to show them. What had I shown them though? They didn't even know why those people had been killed on the highway. To know it was just random violence perpetrated by a lunatic, but that wasn't what I was.

"I had my reasons and that's all I can say, but eventually you'll know the truth," I replied.

It took us another thirty minutes to get to the motel, but all was right with the world because I immediately spotted Melody's brand new Ferrari backed into a corner parking space at the far end of the lot.

"Park beside the Ferrari," I said pointing towards it. Once we came to a stop I took the keys out of the ignition and got out of the car.

"Thank God!" Melody cried, flinging herself from the car into my arms. Holding her tightly and kissing her over and over again, hating myself for the fear that swam in her eyes and caused her body to shake because of it.

"It's okay, I've got you," I whispered in her ear.

"What happened? Are you okay?" she asked, pulling back to inspect me for any type of wound.

"I'm fine, babe, we can talk about it in the room."

"Come on, we're in room one fifteen," she said taking my hand, but she pulled up short when she saw Cindy step out of the car.

"Who…who is that?" Melody asked, looking at me.

"I'll explain it all, come on."

We continued on and Cindy followed behind us, but once we were in the room Melody wanted an explanation with the quickness. I started from the top and ran it all about her, and Cindy added her two cents when appropriate. The look of horror on Melody's face didn't fade until both of us reassured her that I hadn't killed anybody tonight.

"Baby, I'm so proud of you," Melody said pulling me into her arms. I didn't feel like I'd done anything to be proud of, I mean not killing was what all normal people did.

"You understand now why we have to go, right?" I asked her.

"Yes. I have the money and our passports," she said pointing to the bag on the bed.

I hadn't noticed it, but then again I'd been so caught up explaining myself that I hadn't paid attention to anything about the motel room. As long as it had a bed and a shower it would do for the moment.

"How are you feeling?" I asked, rubbing her stomach through the sweatshirt she was wearing.

"I'm fine and the baby is fine so…"

"Baby? You're pregnant?" Cindy asked.

"Yeah," Melody replied hesitantly.

"And you're going on the run? That's not smart, Stephon, and you know that. I told you I can convince my dad not to come after you or file any charges."

"And I told you it's not that simple," I replied through clenched teeth.

"What type of life are you going to have? You're not a street guy, so it's not like you're going to go somewhere and set up

149

shop. You got money now, but how far does that really get a guy with a baby on the way? You were raised by a good man and I bet you want to be every bit of the great father that he was. You can start by giving your child a chance at normalcy and stay here…"

"If we stay here he won't be around to raise his child!" Melody said, frustration causing her voice to raise.

"What? Why?" Cindy asked confused.

When Melody looked up at me I saw all her fears swim to the surface and I felt guilt unlike anything I've known. My decisions had turned her life upside down and that was completely selfish of me. What could I do to fix it though?

"Listen, Cindy, regardless of whether your dad presses charges against me or not I'm still going to be wanted for other things. I did shit I shouldn't have done and because I let you and your family live my cousin, David, is going to turn me in to save himself."

"I…I don't know what to say to that," she replied.

"You don't have to say anything, but now you understand why we have to run. I wouldn't just be going to prison for a few years, it would be a lifetime at best."

"Running is a lifetime too, but it's not just your life. You've got a wife with a baby on the way, and your choice to run is guaranteeing them constant instability. I know that's not what you want," Cindy said shaking her head.

"And how do you know that?"

"Because I know your dad raised you better."

Her words were like a blow to the face and the weight of truth was undeniable. It was funny how people thought about the fucked up decisions they made after they made them, because now I clearly saw all the flaws in my plans. The only question I could ask myself was how to make shit right.

"I'm sorry I got you in this, Cindy," I said giving her the keys to my car. "You can go home."

"What should I do with your car?" she asked.

"Keep it. It was my father's." Even with the keys in her hand she hesitated, but finally she headed for the door.

"Stephon, you're not a bad person, so I think you should ask yourself the tough question. What type of father do you want to be," Cindy said. It was obviously a question that was for me, because before I could open my mouth she was out the door and into the night.

"I can see you thinking, baby, but you made the right decision," Melody said, leading me to the bed where we sat down.

"Baby, I have made so many wrong decisions that I wouldn't know the right one if it landed in my fucking lap."

"It's gonna be okay, Stephon, we'll get through this," she reassured. I believed her, but only because the beginnings of a plan started to formulate in my mind.

"I love you, Melody, and I hope you know that. I know what I have to do."

ASAD

CHAPTER SEVENTEEN

"… And in breaking news, overnight a video was posted on Snap Chat by a man claiming to be responsible for the highway killing. We're coming to you now with that exclusive footage of the shocking confession…"

"A lot of you out there know me because of the tragedy that struck my family last year when my father Stephon Harris Sr. was shot and killed by a Loudoun County police officer. You mourned with me and my family and shared in our outrage when charges were not filed against the officer who pulled the trigger. I sincerely thank each and every one of you who reached out, protested, or took the time to listen when I introduced my father to you via photos and videos. I tried to mourn and accept the loss of my father. I tried to accept that justice could not be served, because a black man's word against a white man doesn't mean shit. I tried. But I was in that car when my dad was shot. I know it was done in cold-blood for no justifiable reason, and knowing that the man who loved me more than life was taken senselessly broke something in me.

"Still, it doesn't excuse my behavior. I felt like black lives wouldn't matter until white people had the chance to feel what we did, to know the fear a black man has every time he leaves his house. So I bought a used cop car, added the authentic touches, and I went on the hunt. I pulled over innocent white people who were unarmed and executed them. Before that, I killed the cop who killed my dad in cold-blood. I also killed another cop outside of Springfield, Virginia who happened upon me trying to kill someone I'd just pulled over.

"I don't say any of this with pride nor will I make excuses for what I've done. My actions were that of a misguided man who thought it was the only way to deal with today's social injustices.

I was wrong. While it's true that black men in America are mistreated, racially profiled, murdered, and thought to be nothing more than second-class citizens, there was nothing I did to help improve any of that. We don't have to fight fire with fire, because we'll get better results by putting the fire out. I wanted to instill fear and change the narrative of the conversation between blacks and whites, but I was missing the bigger picture.

"I'm choosing to come forward now so the real conversation can start about how to fix the racial divide in America. We're all the same. We all need the same oxygen to breathe, and we all bleed the same. We are all the same! If anyone out there can't see the truth in that you have a problem with being yourself. As for those out there that look like me, we have to continue to fight for what we deserve, but we must fight smarter and harder.

"When Willie Lynch gave his speech to the slave masters in Virginia in the 1700s, his message was to keep the niggers ignorant, uneducated, dependent and distrustful of each other. With that promise he helped to kill more black men than Hitler did Jews. Ain't it time for a change? We have to educate ourselves and then each one teach one until we as a collective are no longer ignorant. In order to change the future we have to learn from the past, because if change was impossible then Nigger would still be my name. If slavery didn't break us, then what can? If a black man can be president then what can't a black man do? Perseverance is the key to never give up. I almost did, and in doing that I almost lost myself. That would've made every sacrifice ever made for me one that was done in vain, and I can't allow that because my father raised a better man than that. With that being said I'll be turning myself into the Loudoun County Police Department at 10 AM, because I must pay for the crimes I committed. It's what my father would want."

"...And there you have it folks, Stephon Harris Jr. has taken responsibility for a total of ten homicides beginning with the killing of a police officer. Coming up soon we'll have our legal analyst, Susan Bell, to give her view on the legal ramifications Harris is facing, and we will continue our coverage live from outside the Loudoun County police station. This is Tina Mitchell, Channel 12 news..."

"Is the lawyer meeting us there?" I asked.

"Yeah, my dad said he would, although I'm is not sure what good it will do since you confessed on national TV," Melody replied.

I could tell by the look in her eyes she was still devastated by my decision, but she understood it was something I had to do for her and our baby. There were plenty of men who were fathers from prison and I knew I could do the same. At the end of the day what it came down to was my wife and child deserved a normal life, and if I really loved them I'd want that for them. The road ahead was hard, but at least it was one I could travel with my head held high. That's the man my father raised me to be.

"Mom is gonna meet us there too," I said.

"I know."

"Baby, it's gonna be okay," I said taking her hand.

All she could do was nod as more tears sprang from her already red eyes. I knew nothing I could say would stop the tears. Even when we made love for the last time at sunrise she cried in silent waves that shattered my heart.

"Come on, we gotta go," I said standing up and pulling her to her feet.

Walking outside into the morning sunlight I tried to take it all in and savor the last moments of freedom I would probably ever know. I held onto Melody's hand, needing her strength if I was gonna go through with this.

ASAD

"You drive," she said passing me her keys. She put the bag of money in the trunk and got in the passenger seat.

"Not a bad way to go to prison, huh?" I said climbing behind the wheel and firing the engine.

I was hoping my comment would get even a slight smile out of her, but her face remained contorted in sadness. Our ride was a silent one, but I took comfort in knowing that despite it all, she was right by my side where I needed her to be. Before I knew it I was pulling up in the familiar parking lot of the police station, but it felt like it had been a different lifetime since I was here last.

"It's an absolute fucking circus," Melody said.

"That's putting it mildly," I said, looking around in shock at how many people were out here both in front of the police station and across the street.

There were signs being waved calling me a murderer and serial killer, and there were others demanding my freedom. It was crazy.

"I don't want you to get out of the car with me," I said.

"Stephon, I'm going with you..."

"Baby, if that mob rushes me and something happens to you or our child I could never forgive myself. Please just let me do this and you can come in once things calm down a little."

I knew she wanted to be with me every step of the way, but she would respect my need to keep her and the baby safe. When she kissed me I felt every ounce of love she had in her soul for what we shared, and I knew I'd made the right decision in sacrificing my life for theirs.

"I love you more than life itself," I said, taking her face in my hands so we were only a breath away.

"I love you too, baby."

I kissed her one more time and then I opened the car door and stepped out. I took off my hoodie and my t-shirt, figuring that walking up shirtless so they could see I didn't have any weapons

156

was to my benefit. With one final look at Melody I began the longest walk of my life. As soon as the first camera crew spotted me the world lit up with flashes and a million questions were coming my way. I could see the outrage on a lot of faces in the crowd, some white, some black, but at least they finally had something to agree on.

Despite being swarmed, I continued to make my way towards the police station, not answering any questions along the way. When I was finally on the police department's property, I raised my hands high and shouted that I was unarmed. I could see the police coming out the front doors toward me, but I suddenly felt the force of a sledgehammer hit me in the back right before I heard the roar of thunder. I tried to hold my arms out in front of me to slow my impact on the concrete, but my brain didn't translate the signal fast enough and I went down face first.

The screams around me were deafening and I could feel the earth shaking with the pounding footsteps of everyone moving at once. I didn't understand what was going on. But then the pain started. It felt like my chest was on fire, literally, and I couldn't seem to catch my breath. My mind was screaming at me to move because I'd been shot, but my body wouldn't comply. It wasn't until I started to taste copper that the real fear set in and kept me company, and it was in no hurry to go away. I opened my mouth to speak, but nothing came out except a cough that left the sidewalk stained bright red.

I could feel everything around me happening so fast, but it felt like time was standing still all in the same instant. Was this the end? Were the credits rolling on the short film of my life? I didn't know. The only thing I did know was that where justice fails karma fulfills. Not even I was exempt from that…

To Be Continued…

157

ASAD

Coming Soon from Lock Down Publications/Ca$h Presents

TORN BETWEEN TWO

By **Coffee**

LAST OF A DYING BREED

LAY IT DOWN **III**

By **Jamaica**

BLOOD OF A BOSS **IV**

By **Askari**

BRIDE OF A HUSTLA **III**

By **Destiny Skai**

WHEN A GOOD GIRL GOES BAD **II**

By **Adrienne**

LOVE & CHASIN' PAPER **II**

By **Qay Crockett**

I RIDE FOR MY HITTA **II**

By **Misty Holt**

THE HEART OF A GANGSTA **II**

By **Jerry Jackson**

TO DIE IN VAIN **II**

By **ASAD**

Available Now

RESTRAING ORDER **I & II**

By **CA$H & Coffee**

LOVE KNOWS NO BOUNDARIES **I II & III**

By **Coffee**

LAY IT DOWN **I & II**

By **Jamaica**

PUSH IT TO THE LIMIT

By **Bre' Hayes**

BLOOD OF A BOSS **I II & III**

By **Askari**

THE STREETS BLEED MURDER **I, II & III**

THE HEART OF A GANGSTA

By **Jerry Jackson**

CUM FOR ME

An **LDP Erotica Collaboration**

BRIDE OF A HUSTLA **I II**

By **Destiny Skai**

WHEN A GOOD GIRL GOES BAD

By **Adrienne**

A GANGSTER'S REVENGE **I II III & IV**

By **Aryanna**

WHAT ABOUT US **I & II**

NEVER LOVE AGAIN

THUG ADDICTION

By **Kim Kaye**

THE KING CARTEL **I, II & III**

By **Frank Gresham**

THESE NIGGAS AIN'T LOYAL **I, II & III**

By **Nikki Tee**

GANGSTA SHYT **I II &II**I

By **CATO**

THE ULTIMATE BETRAYAL

By **Phoenix**

DON'T FU#K WITH MY HEART **I & II**

By **Linnea**

BOSS'N UP **I & II**

By **Royal Nicole**

I LOVE YOU TO DEATH

By Destiny J

I RIDE FOR MY HITTA

By **Misty Holt**

LOVE & CHASIN' PAPER

By **Qay Crockett**

<u>BOOKS BY LDP'S CEO, CA$H</u>

TRUST NO MAN

TRUST NO MAN 2

TRUST NO MAN 3

BONDED BY BLOOD

SHORTY GOT A THUG

A DIRTY SOUTH LOVE

THUGS CRY

THUGS CRY 2

TRUST NO BITCH

TRUST NO BITCH 2

TRUST NO BITCH 3

TIL MY CASKET DROPS

RESTRAINING ORDER

RESTRAINING ORDER 2

<u>Coming Soon</u>

TRUST NO BITCH (KIAM EYEZ' STORY)

THUGS CRY 3

BONDED BY BLOOD 2

IN LOVE WITH HIS GANGSTA

Stay Connected with Us!

Text **LOCKDOWN** to 22828 to stay up-to-date with new releases, sneak peaks, contests and more...

Made in the USA
Columbia, SC
30 March 2021